Archie Judd was sick—
too sick to see any visitors

He just lay in his bed in the old Judd mansion and gave orders.

Barney Kains was Judd's ghost artist. He drew Judd's comic strip while the old artist was ill. Kains had always longed to meet Archie Judd, but somehow he had never been able to.

And then one day Kains found himself alone in the Judd house. He went exploring, determined to meet his idol face to face.

And then—shockingly—he did!

GHOSTING

Ron Goulart

A RAVEN HOUSE MYSTERY FROM

WORLDWIDE
TORONTO • LONDON • NEW YORK • SYDNEY

Raven House edition published March 1982

Second printing March 1982

ISBN 0-373-63025-5

Printed in Canada

1

His wife was all over the place.

Former wife, actually; legally separated wife. Manhattan-based now, meteorically rising wife. She confronted him on the covers of *People*, *Time*, *Mammon*, *Us*, *Cosmopolitan*, the *National Intruder*, etc. The most successful model in America, looking absolutely stunning, compellingly gaunt, sparsely clothed, red hair glowing like a beacon.

"Poetic fancy can do you in," Barney Kains warned himself aloud, gathering up the magazines and tabloids off his rickety coffee table, after first turning them facedown, and lugging the batch across the small living room of his cottage. He tossed them all into a cluttered closet, shut the door quickly so they wouldn't get out. "When you start having poetic fancies about your ex-wife, you're only one step from baying at the moon."

He missed one tabloid. The *Intruder* was still staring at him from his lopsided sofa. There was his erstwhile spouse flashing the incredible slightly puckered smile that was provocative enough to raise the dead. Over her lovely head blazed the line "Tawny Tells of U.F.O. Ride!"

"She never told me she went riding in one of those things." Barney, a tall lean man of thirty-one, loped over to his television set to flick it on. "C'mon, distract me."

And there she was. Long legs gleaming, emerald eyes ablaze, saying, "It's the only sensible way to live, Mike. I mean, being a vegetarian means a great—"

"You're not a goddamned vegetarian!" Barney yelled at her image. "You're one of the most carnivorous people I've ever known. Who ate bacon sandwiches in bed? Not me."

"That's absolutely fascinating, Tawny," said Mike Douglas.

Sure, it was. She could tell you she had an ingrown toenail and you'd be fascinated. Face it, she was a very fascinating woman.

"Shit," remarked Barney as he killed the picture.

A heavy spring rain was pounding on the slanted roof of his cottage this afternoon, slapping at the small windows. He listened to that for a spell, found it didn't distract him.

Barney went wandering into his studio, avoiding his drawing board. He knew what lay in wait for him there.

His cottage, which he rented for twice its worth, stood at the edge of a ten-acre estate.

The kindly old widowed light-industry millionaire up at the main house sent him down all his used magazines, figuring an artist ought to keep up with the world.

He strived to focus on the world, but got sidetracked by images of Tawny.

"You should've known you were in trouble the minute she first told you her name," he said to himself as he inched nearer the drawing board. "It's her real damn name. Her mother and father actually trooped into a church in St. Paul, Minnesota, twenty-six years ago to tack it on her. That's such a clear-cut sign of hereditary insanity you should've spotted it right off."

Hell, he'd have married her if her name had been Minerva Urecal or Typhoid Mary. Barney was afraid that if Tawny suddenly came back into his life he'd marry her again.

"Argh!" He'd forced himself to look at what was on his drawing board.

Sometimes, after the fires of creation had cooled, the garbage you'd turned out didn't look quite so garbagesque. No such luck this time.

He settled, uneasily, into his padded chair. There was the Human Beast kicking the crap out of a gang of Lobstermen. *Slop!* and *Splong!* was lettered everywhere. And, God help him, there was considerable saliva drooling out of the lobster fellows' mouths.

Barney'd thought about phoning the reference room at the Westport Library to ask if lobsters really salivated. He'd decided against it, realizing nobody up at Maximus Comics, Inc., would care. They liked saliva anyway. Doted on it, in fact.

"A look at my view," he reminded himself, pushing back from the drawing board. "That'll soothe me."

He headed back into the living room, aiming for the window that provided a look at the Sound. He never reached the view, discovering himself instead crouched before the television set and furtively turning it back on.

". . . carrots, Mike. I completely love and admire carrots and, umm, are they good for you."

"That's absolutely fascinating, Tawny."

"You never ate a carrot in your life!" accused Barney. "Your idea of a balanced meal was pizza with a side order of fries."

But, God, she did look great. She'd managed to cross her incredible legs in a fantastic new way, seeming to be all tan and creamy thighs. Thighs and cleavage.

How the hell could Mike Douglas sit there so blithely?

Sighing, he forced himself to turn off the set. He remained staring at the tiny dot that had been his former wife.

His problem was worse than anything the Human Beast had ever had to face. All that happened to him was he turned into a big blue shaggy monster whenever he got really pissed off. But Beast never had to worry about still being hot for the wife who'd completely walked out on him four and a half months ago.

There wasn't a chance in the world she'd ever—

His phone rang.

Might just be her. Sure, the Douglas show was on tape.

He dashed back to his studio, grabbed the phone receiver up off the taboret. "You look terrific," he blurted.

"Thanks, old buddy. You're cute, too, and just wait until the videophone gets here and you can get a real good look at me." It was Ty Banner.

"I was anticipating someone else, Ty."

"You've got to snap out of this obsession, old buddy," advised Banner, whose voice was deep, and slightly blurred most of the time. "I have, by curious coincidence, exactly the thing to yank you out of the doldrums."

"Doubtful."

"You know my third wife, of course."

"Is she the one you've got now?"

"Yes, name of Trish."

"I know her, met her with you at Zarley's party last month."

"Trish's got the Omaha Flu."

"That's too bad," said Barney, trying not to look down at what he'd drawn on page 11 of the

latest seventeen-page Human Beast episode.
"Or is it? I've never heard of that particular flu.
Could be it makes you euphorically happy, fills
your life with—"

"It gives you the trots," explained Banner.
"Trish seems to be, according to Dr. Strump,
the first person in Connecticut to have it. She's
always been something of a trendsetter."

"Did you want medical advice from me or
sympathy or what?"

"No, I'm scheduled to attend the annual
Newspaper Artists Guild banquet this very
night, old buddy," Banner continued. "I have
two ducats, as we used to call them along the
Gay White Way, back when it was still okay to
be gay. Damn things cost forty-five bucks
apiece and are nonreturnable. Now, from a
logistical point of view, it's impossible to take a
wife who's got the runs to a posh banquet at the
posh Hotel Babylon in Manhattan."

"That makes sense, still I—"

"So why don't you come along instead? My
treat."

"Naw, I'm not a newspaper cartoonist. I'm
only a defrocked commercial illustrator who got
dragooned into the comic-book business."

"You're a gifted artist, old buddy," Banner
told him, almost seriously. "If you'd get your
head out of your ass and quit moping over
Tawny, you'd be back doing book covers and
high-price ads in no time."

"Doubtful."

"Look, it's a proven fact that recluses never have any fun," said his cartoonist friend. "A ton of self-pity and a dime'll buy you three minutes on the phone. You'll mingle with the greats and the near greats at this N.A.G. banquet, not to mention a bevy of nifty ladies."

"Don't own a tux, too late to rent one."

"You don't need formal attire, old buddy. Simply don that sincere gray suit you use on interviews."

"I'm not exactly ready for society yet. Actually I think I ought to mope for a—"

"I'm up for the Katzie tonight, you know."

"No, I'd forgotten."

"My peers may have voted 'Dr. Judge's Family' the Best Continuity Strip of the year once again. Amid loud acclaim and enthusiastic applause I may—only a few hours from now—stumble up to the podium to accept that gilded little statue of the Katzenjammer Kids that represents the highest honor—"

"Okay, okay, if there's a possibility of seeing something as heartwarming as that, I guess I'll come." Barney realized that if he stuck home tonight he'd be haunted by Tawny and all those tantalizing images of her he had stuffed away in the closet. Better to escape into reality for a few hours.

"Splendid, old buddy." Banner chuckled approvingly into the phone. "I want a lot of spontaneous applause. If I do win the frigging dornick, you can lead that."

"I'll clap with both hands, Ty," promised Barney. "You going into the city on the train?"

"Right. Can you meet me at the Westport Station in time to catch the 5:35?"

"It'll mean leaving the Human Beast at the mercy of several mean-minded lobsters, but I think so. Yeah."

Banner said, "I may have someone to introduce you to once we arrive at the Babylon."

"Like whom?"

"I'll explain later," said Banner. "This someone could well be the person to get you out of your rut. Could even change your life."

Which turned out to be absolutely true.

2

"WHERE?"

"Way across the ballroom, old buddy, just between Milt Caniff and that marble pillar."

"I don't see her. Not that fat lady who looks like an unsuccessful bulldog?"

"Christ, Barney, that's Hulda Glackens, the comics editor up at Expedient Features Syndicate," said Ty Banner. He was a tall, traditionally handsome man of fifty-six with a few too many wrinkles and pouches on his tanned face. "I mean that petite brunette."

Barney, clad in his sincere interview suit, squinted. There were about four hundred people crowded into this ballroom of the Babylon, mingling, milling, using the two long makeshift cocktail bars. "I don't see her," he said. "Petite? Does that mean she's flat-chested?"

"It means she's not six feet tall like your late wife." Banner paused to sip his Scotch. "Listen, I'm not trying to pimp or procure, this is a strictly legit business setup. Something, I think, that'll take your mind off that flagpole Tawny and get you out of the grip of Maximus Comics, as well. For a while anyway. You can't spend the rest of your life whacking off over magazine pics of your onetime wife and batting out the likes of the Human Beast.''

''They've promised me I'll be taking over Captain Cyclops, too.'' Barney tilted, still trying to get a glimpse of the girl his friend was anxious for him to meet. ''That's Captain Cyclops, the One-Eyed Wonder.''

''Do you know what 'Poor Little Pearl' nets the Judd family each and every year?''

''A million bucks.''

''Not quite, but almost. And I know for a.... Hi, Jerry. Strip's looking great. That was Jerry Robinson.''

Barney said, ''Okay, they make near a million. That doesn't mean they'll offer a ghost artist like me more than a couple of hundred a week.''

''Bethany Judd is a nice kid,'' Banner assured him. ''Hey, Alfred. You're very dapper, as always. There's Alfred Andriola, over by the velvet drapes.''

Nodding absently at the distant little cartoonist, Barney said, ''So she's got a pleasant personality, on top of being so petite. That doesn't have much to do with what they'll offer me. I hear Archie Judd is a tightfisted old bastard.''

''He's cautious with a buck,'' admitted Banner after another swallow of Scotch. ''Here's the setup. Archie, incredible as it may seem, draws and letters the whole damn strip unaided. Imagine that, daily and Sunday all by himself since 1929. I think in all that time he's only had a couple of assistants and nobody at all for the past few years. His son, Russell Judd, scripts the strip and manages the business end. You've probably heard there's a Broadway musical and a TV series in the works. Fifty percent of all that'll go to the syndicate, of course, but the rest is going to be Archie Judd's.''

''I don't see that the life of a ghost is much better than that of an employee of Maximus, Ty.''

''We're not talking, as I explained to you on the train coming in, about being Archie Judd's ghost for the rest of your natural life. From what Beth has told me . . . and she's sort of the general handyperson on the strip . . . the old boy is down with some kind of respiratory thing. When you're nearly eighty, that can knock you out for a spell. So they figure he'll be out of the picture for maybe a month or two at most, that's how long they'll need help.''

''Well, I do need some extra dough right about now,'' said Barney slowly. ''The legal fees from all this business with Tawny are—''

''Holy moley, what a surprise.'' Someone nudged Barney in the small of the back. ''Aren't you the guy who was once wed to that fabled titian-haired model person?''

"Texaco." Barney spun around to grin at Juan Texaco.

The small curly-haired artist laughed. "Your period of mourning over?"

"I'm able to sit up and take nourishment." He surveyed his friend. "Is that a tuxedo?"

"So I've been led to believe. Gives me that dapper Roger Moore look, no?"

"A foreshortened Roger Moore, yeah. How come you're here at all, Texaco?"

"Maximus Comics always buys six tickets," he replied. "Carlotsky is down with the Wichita Flu and he let me—"

"You mean the Omaha Flu."

"No, this is much worse than that." Texaco took Barney's arm, led him over against a flocked wall. "Listen, are you planning to give up the Human Beast?"

"No, I'm fervently dedicated to the character." He frowned. "Hell, I've spent the week learning to draw lobstermen, so I'm not about to quit. Why?"

"Carlotsky asked me to stand by to take over," said his friend. "Meaning I may have to drop Flaming Death."

"You think Carlotsky's unhappy with my stuff?"

"Carlotsky hasn't been happy with anything since an Erector Set he got when he was six." Texaco scanned the fluctuating crowd. "Isn't that Dorothy Lamour over there patting Irwin Hasen on the head?"

"No."

"Did I tell you about the girl who assaulted me on the subway last week? She looked exactly like Arlene Dahl, only younger. Confided in me she's always had an overwhelming yen to commit the vilest kind of sexual indiscretions with a diminutive Cuban built along my lines. I modestly explained that—"

"Are my days numbered up at Maximus? Carlotsky's promised me a hike to eighty-five dollars a page, you know."

"This is like asking if I think they'll let you reenlist in the French Foreign Legion," the curlyheaded cartoonist answered. "You're better off out of that place."

"I'm out?"

"I didn't say that. Who knows what's on Carlotsky's mind besides fungus and old bits of twine. That sure looks like Bonita Granville over there. Did I inform you about this girl who made a very successful grab at certain of my intimate parts while I was window-shopping in front of—"

"I need this damn job with Maximus."

"No, you don't. No more than you need an African ceremonial sword inserted up your butt," said Texaco. "This girl who couldn't refrain from fondling me in front of Barnes & Noble bore an uncanny resemblance to the Sylvia Sydney of the 1930s. Soulful, yet sexy, dark and—"

"They didn't have old movies in Cuba, did

they? How come your mind is a sink of old actresses?''

"It's genetic. During the thirties and forties
my late father worked up here as a doorman at
a movie palace in Yonkers," explained Texaco.
"Ah, there's Beth Judd. Hi, Beth. Very cute
girl.''

Barney whirled to gaze in the direction of
Texaco's grinning nod. He saw nothing but
backs. "You know her?"

"She's a very nice person, which is one rea-
son I've never succeeded with her," he said.
"She respects me as an artist, but not a man.
Hey, that's got to be Ruth Roman hugging Stan
Drake over there under the crystal chandelier."

"What's Beth Judd like?"

"Petite.''

"Beyond that.''

"Sweet, wholesome, attractive—at least to us
Latinos with dangerous upward mobility ten-
dencies," Texaco elaborated. "Why the sudden
interest in her?''

"Friend of mine was suggesting I might be
able to do some free-lance work for Archie
Judd. She's the one who told him about the job
coming up.''

Texaco laughed. "Ah, I see the whole vast
conspiracy. It might work, too," he said.
"Sweet Bethany makes you forget the sulky
Tawny Kains, gets you out of your slough of
despond, away from the clutches of Maximus

and back into the mainstream of crass commercialism. Yep, it ought to work fine.''

"I'm not looking to get pulled out of any sloughs or into any affairs right now," Barney told him. "I'm not even considering leaving Maximus Comics, Inc. Although maybe Carlotsky has different ideas.''

"Naw, he won't drop you. Although he might switch you to *Peter Pupp Comics*, knowing of your flair for whimsy.''

"Funny-animal stuff? He's threatening to stick me on one of the few funny-animal mags left in America?''

Texaco lowered his curly head, fussed with his lacy cuffs. "I wasn't supposed to reveal that to you, Barn," he said. "But that is what the human beast of editordom is seriously contemplating for you.''

"Shit.''

"Agreed," said Texaco. "So why not say goodbye to all that and go to work for Beth and her folks? She's really a very striking young woman. Has to be or she couldn't have picked up those TV-commercial jobs she's—''

"Whoa, wait. Beth Judd is an actress? A model?''

"Aspiring actress, yep. She's done a handful of television spots over the past couple years. You probably saw her on the one for Lady Litewait Sanitary Pads, if you watch the Late Show with any dedication. Opens with Beth and this

terrific blonde who is a dead ringer for Martha
O'Driscoll playing a fast set of tennis and then
Beth says, 'Tell me, Alicia, how is it you always
manage to beat me and look so cool and comfortable even on those days when—' ''

"Damn, an actress. One step from being a
model."

"C'mon, she's not at all like Tawny. If that's
what is causing you to blanch and tremble."

"I don't want to get involved with any more
women who have show-business aspirations.
Even in a strictly business way."

"You'll actually be working for her crusty old
granddad."

"An actress, wow."

"What say we push over to the bar for another drink," suggested the little cartoonist.

"Trouble, that's all they are. Actresses,
models, stunt women." He began wedging his
way toward the nearest bar, Texaco following
in his wake. "It's an ego thing."

"Nonsense. I have a monstrous ego and yet I
remain the prince of good fellows. I was re-
marking, only last evening, on this very topic to
a stunning girl I encountered at the Cuba Libre
Disco. And she looked so much like Maria
Montez that it'd curl your—"

"I'd almost come in and work full-time in the
Maximus bull pen," said Barney, "rather than
go into a damn situation where there is an aspiring actress underfoot."

"Well, join me in the bull pen then, Barn. They've got plenty of Peter Pupp awaiting you."

"How come, so late in life, I'm still hung up with such junky alternatives?" asked Barney.

After several seconds with no reply Barney looked back over his shoulder. Instead of Texaco he saw a lanky woman in a nearly frontless dress, holding a martini glass in each hand.

"I'm Cuz Marino's wife, Chicago Examiner Syndicate," she smiled.

"Oh, sure. How's old Cuz?" Barney had never heard of Cuz Marino and wasn't even too sure about the Chicago Examiner.

"As well as can be expected. It looks like it wasn't as malignant as we . . . ."

She was swallowed by the crowd and Barney continued barward alone. Suddenly he arrived at a clearing in the forest of people. Already in it were a pretty slender dark-haired girl and a lumbering young man in a plaid dinner jacket.

"It's not that at all, Jape," the girl was saying, struggling quietly to get free of the tight grip he had on her bare, tan arm.

"Like hell. You're letting the fact I jumped you cloud your commercial sense, sweet. You know damn well I can handle any—"

"There's nothing to handle. Now, please, unhook yourself from me."

"I can work in any style, you know that."

The girl, lips pressed tight, pushed her free

hand against the big blond guy's frilly chest, shoving.

He kept his hold, pulling her closer.

"The lady'd like you to let go of her," Barney found himself saying in a voice several shades deeper than his usual one.

What late movie idol was that borrowed from? John Wayne? Jake Troop? Dick Powell?

"Huh?" Jape scowled back over his wide shoulder, broad flat face flushed and perspiring.

"Let her go."

"Who the crap do you think you might be?"

"Just the guy who's going to knock you on your keister if you don't oblige."

Odd. Barney had never been the brawl type. Something, though, about seeing this lout clutching this particular girl inspired him, transformed him.

"Thanks," the dark girl said to him. "Although now he's probably going to try something nasty on you, too."

"We samaritans are used to that. Hey, let go."

Jape let go, turned his now free hand into a large fist. He jerked it back, readying a punch.

Somebody caught the hand, and spun Jape around. Someone else took hold of his shoulder. They were big men, both older than he. "Stop being an asshole, Jape," one of them advised as they hustled him away from there.

"Thanks again," said the girl.

"You okay?"

She smoothed at the front of her dark cocktail dress. "Yes, fine."

"That was Jape Easter, wasn't it?"

"Yes. You're not a friend of his."

"Nor an admirer of his work. Seen him around Westport a few times is all."

"Oh, do you—"

"You darling child." A husky old woman with blue hair popped out of the crowd to hug the slim girl.

Her knobby cane was hooked on her puffy, mottled left arm and its ferrule managed to whack Barney a good one in the knee.

By the time he'd murmured, "Oof," she'd taken the rescued brunette off into the swarm.

"Here you are." Banner caught hold of him. "Let's hasten yonder, old buddy, to where I've got Russ Judd eagerly waiting to chat with you. I told him you were a bloody genius, so try not to stand there with your lower lip slack."

"I was just almost in a fight, Ty."

"That's what these N.A.G. affairs are for. Come along."

He led Barney through a labyrinth of tuxedos, dark suits, cocktail dresses and party gowns to a relatively uncluttered patch of red carpet near a crystal wall lamp.

A small balding man of fifty-five was standing there. He was pale, sad eyed behind his rimless glasses, and he was frowning at the cigarette between his fingers, as though mildy surprised to see it smoldering there. Putting it out in an urn ashtray, he held out a hand to Banner. "You always look so damn fit, Ty."

"Golf and expensive booze work wonders. Russ Judd, this is Barney Kains."

Judd's hand was cold, damp. "I hear you might be interested in helping us out," he said.

"Well, I'd have to know quite a bit more about the situation first." If Beth looked anything like her father, her acting career was doomed.

Judd coughed into his hand. "I can't understand why I keep smoking, it's so self-destructive," he said. "Well, we're in something of a bind on the strip, Mr. Kains. Nothing serious, but dad's under the weather and we think it's best he rest up for a few weeks. The doctor advises us he ought to lay his pen aside until he's completely well." Judd managed a small tight smile up at Banner and Barney. "You can imagine how dad took the news, since he's a real demon for work. And the strip is his life."

Nodding, Banner said, "I haven't seen Archie in more than a year. He hardly gets out at all anymore, does he?"

"Socially, no. But he insists on cycling. He's kept that up, does two miles every morning rain or shine." Judd shook his head in mild amusement over his father. "Dad gets up every single morning at six, Mr. Kains, and heads for those twisting lanes up behind our estate. Incredible dedication, and he swears it's what keeps him young."

"If I were you, Russ, I'd get a bike and follow him to make sure.... Hi, Orlando. Saw your gag in *Good Housekeeping*."

While Banner moved off to talk with someone else, Judd eased closer to Barney.

"Ty assures me you can imitate dad's style."

"I'm pretty good at that sort of thing. Last year I ghosted a couple weeks of 'Dr. Judge's Family' for Ty when he went to Mexico on vacation."

"He also tells me you're one of the best young artists in the East."

"I'm a damn good commercial artist," Barney admitted. "Cartooning I fell into when some of my commercial art accounts dried up."

"The work you do in the Maximus books is quite good."

Barney blinked. "You see that stuff?"

A small thin smile. "I keep up with all the competition, Mr. Kains. Comic books, all other strips, books, movies, television. 'Poor Little Pearl' has been a very valuable property for more than fifty years. We intend to keep it that way."

"You seem to be succeeding. I hear there's a musical in the works and a possible series."

"Yes, those are just about set."

"Excuse my asking," Barney said. "But does your father own 'Poor Little Pearl'?"

After a few seconds hesitation, Judd replied, "Unfortunately, no, Mr. Kains. As you probably know, almost no newspaper syndicate will give the creator of a strip ownership. It's rather a nineteenth-century way of doing things, but there it is. I will say, however, that Independent Features has always been extremely open and fair with us. We receive fifty percent of all profits from 'Pearl.' "

"I guess that is sort of generous. Up at Maximus it's page rates and that's it."

"We're going to need help on the strip almost at once," continued Judd, voice lowering. "Dad—workhorse that he is—is ten weeks ahead of deadline on the dailies and thirteen on the Sundays. In order to maintain that schedule the substitute work will have to start very soon now."

"Suppose I give it a try," said Barney, "what sort of money are we talking about?"

"If you're satisfactory, and I'm certain you will be, we can offer you six hundred dollars. All I'd like to see first is a couple of sample dailies."

"Six hundred a week?"

Another small smile. "Of course."

That would mean twenty-four hundred dollars a month. If Barney could do the strip for a while, and hold onto the Maximus chores, as well, his income stood to take a great leap forward. It'd be nothing like Tawny's, but more than sufficient for him. "Well, okay, I think I can—"

"Russ, how the hell are you?" A large shaggy man, open faced and jovial, had come pushing through the crowd to them.

"I'm fine, Jocko. But I hear you're not. Sorry about the museum."

"Could've been a heck of a lot worse." The big man scanned the immediate crowd. "Archie not here?"

Judd said, "He wasn't feeling quite up to it."

"His hand worse?"

"Hand?"

"Didn't Archie tell you he dropped in at the museum last week—last Monday? Fortunately it was before the damn storeroom went up in flames. So he got a look at the originals."

Frowning, Judd said, "Yes, I knew about the jaunt. That young fanatic, Folger, insisted on dragging him out. One of the rare trips he makes these days, but Folger insisted Archie had to see the old 'Pearl' Sunday-page originals you'd acquired in that new collection you bought for the museum."

"Good thing he did. That was part of what burned up in our damn fire," said the big man. "I noticed when Archie was there that he had a bandage on his drawing hand."

"Oh, that was nothing. A fall from his bike,

which is something else we can't talk him out of," said Judd. "About your fire, how much damage was done?"

"That part of the Graphic Arts Museum holdings was insured for five hundred thousand dollars, Russ. You know, that was one of the best collections of comic-art originals turned up in this country in years. Hell, we had Winsor McKay, Herriman, Foster 'Tarzan' pages, Milt Gross, Gibson, all the greats. Lots of people still don't realize how valuable original comic art can be. They were heavily insured but I can't ever buy another collection of originals like that. An original, after all, is a one-of-a-kind thing. I even had three Heinrich Kley drawings in the warehouse when it burned. Beautiful stuff, with those fantastic animals of his dancing with naked ladies."

Judd said, "By the way, Mr. Kains, do you know Jocko Pease?"

"Only his work." Barney held out his hand.

Shaking it enthusiastically, Pease chuckled. "My work? Hell, I haven't done a panel for more than two years. And before that last one folded I was down to a dozen papers. You'd have had to haunt out-of-town newspaper dealers to keep up with me," he said. "I was ready to go back to assisting or ghosting when I got the idea for the Graphic Arts Museum, and found enough backing from friends of my wife."

"When was the fire?" asked Barney. "I hadn't heard about it."

"Last Wednesday, not quite a week ago." Pease shook his head forlornly. "All that beautiful artwork up in smoke—what a pain." He gazed around at the milling crowd again. "So Archie isn't feeling well?"

"Touch of the flu, nothing to worry about," answered Judd.

"He's a great old guy. I hope it doesn't turn into anything serious."

"He'll be back at the board in no time. We practically had to tie him down to get him to spend even a day in bed."

"If you need any help, just get on the horn," offered the shaggy-headed Pease. "I've ghosted for the best of 'em."

"I don't think it'll come to that, Jocko, but thanks."

Pease nodded a few times. "Hey, there's Lennie Starr, got to talk to him about 'Annie.' Nice meeting you, Barney. Specially since you're a fan of mine." Laughing, he shoved into the crowd.

"I've never been too fond of Jocko," admitted Judd after a few seconds. "He's not someone I'd pick out to help in a situation like the present one. And he's far from being the most discreet man in the business."

"Too bad about the museum, though. I've been meaning to get over to Southport to look around."

"Now as to our—"

"Has he agreed, pop?"

Barney turned and saw the girl he'd just recently helped rescue. "You're Beth Judd," he said with a grin.

"I never did thank you sufficiently." She smiled at him. "So thanks."

"You've already met," realized Judd. "I've outlined our problem to Mr. Kains, Bethany, and made him an offer. But, in all the confusion, I'm not certain of his answer."

"It was yes," said Barney, eyes on the girl.

THE LAST TRAIN for Westport, Connecticut, would be leaving in twenty minutes at 12:35 A.M. Grand Central Station had a slow, sleepy feel to it, nearly everything was shut down and shuttered. A black clean-up man was nudging an empty cigarette package across the vast marble floor with a push broom. A gray-bearded old man in two overcoats was hunting, with great concentration, through a trash container.

"There's last year's winner," said Ty Banner as he came down the marble steps from the Vanderbilt Street entrance. He was carrying a porcelain statuette of two squat boys carefully in front of him.

"Don't minimize the honor," cautioned Barney. "It's always good to get recognition from your peers."

"They could've given me a box to keep this damn thing in," complained Banner about his just-won award. "Even an old brown paper bag. Feel like an idiot boarding the train clutching an effigy of Hans and Fritz Katzenjammer.''

"I'll carry it."

"I don't feel that foolish." He glanced up at the immense schedule board. "Our train's leaving on track thirteen. That doesn't sound like good luck."

"Give me a dollar," demanded a wild-eyed young man who jumped into their path. He was clad in a ruined tweed sport coat, khaki trousers and ski boots.

"Be gone," advised Banner.

"I'm starving, I want to eat."

"You look like a boozer or a junkie to me," said Banner.

"Least I don't play with dolls, you snotty mother."

Barney slipped the twitchy young man a crumpled dollar bill. "Here."

"Thanks. God bless you." He jammed the money away inside his coat someplace and went tottering off.

"Sappo," said Banner.

"Probably so."

They continued on toward the train gateway they wanted.

"Did you ever wonder," asked Banner after a moment, "which one is Hans and which one is Fritz?"

"Nope."

"The dark-haired one is Fritz, the blondie is Hans."

"That's a pile of crap, mister." A blotch-faced woman who'd been feeling in phone slots for forgotten change had overheard their passing conversation and was walking sideways beside them.

"You're telling, my good woman, the recipient of the prestigious Katzie Award that he doesn't know Hans Katzenjammer from Fritz Katzenjammer?"

"I doubt you even know crap from shinola," she said. "Fritz is the blond one, everybody with any sense knows that. Why are you lugging that dumb thing around anyhow?"

"It's an award."

"From a penny arcade?"

Banner replied, "In a manner of speaking, yes."

"Well, best of luck." She scurried off to another bank of pay phones.

"The honors keep heaping up on me," said Banner.

Gate thirteen was already open and they went down the stairway to the train platform.

At the foot of the stairs a plump middle-aged man in a dark topcoat was sitting fanning himself with a copy of *The Playbill*. His wife, a thin, sad-faced woman, was urging him to get up. "I should've known when you didn't come back from the second act intermission you were going to end up like this, Biff."

"Can't stand British farces," mumbled Biff.

"Curse of drink," observed Banner. "I like to sit in the very head car, old buddy. Dana Fradon tells me that's the most dangerous car on the whole train, but I am fond of riding home aboard it."

"I've been thinking some more about this ghosting business, Ty," Barney said.

"It's a damn good deal, working for the Judds," his friend told him. "They're honest people, which I don't have to remind you, old pal, is a rarity in our noble profession. Salary isn't bad either."

"I can use the extra six hundred a week, and I told them I'd try out for the job," he said as they walked along the platform tunnel in the chill night. "I keep wondering if I'm just getting myself into another rut, some place I'm going to want to get away from in a while."

"You are, yes." Banner brought his award statue up closer to his eyes. "That whey-faced bimbo may've been dead right, now I think on it. The towheaded lad is Fritz, the other one is Hans. My advice, old buddy, is accept the job if they like your samples. You're not committing yourself to a lifelong. . . Barney?"

Barney was stopped beside one of the lighted Conrail passenger cars, gazing inside. "Hum?"

"Why this sudden trance state? You didn't drink anything but sparkling water at the banquet."

Inside the car, near one of the exit doors, was

a large poster. It showed an incredibly lovely young woman coming, dripping and bikini-clad, out of some Florida surf. It was Tawny.

"Never saw this one before," Barney explained, squinting slightly. "She's tan all over. Every inch of her. Sometimes I—"

"Come along, Barney." Getting hold of him by the arm, Banner tugged. "Let's go sit in the death car, where you can struggle to get over this latest attack."

Barney took a deep breath. "I'm okay, Ty. Sorry." They resumed walking. "You made a dandy acceptance speech, I thought."

"I may have spoiled it a bit by giggling," said Banner. "What's this I hear about you and that lout, Jape Easter, trading punches."

"Nope, actually we only threatened to do violence to each other."

"Do you want to sit backward or frontward?" asked Banner, stepping through the open doorway of the head passenger car.

"Doesn't matter."

"I like to face forward, so I can see any impending head-on collisions in plenty of time." He edged up the aisle. "We'll take this seat for three. You don't mind if I let the Katzenjammer Kids sit between us."

After they were all seated Barney said, "What's the tie-in between Easter and Bethany?"

"He's an abandoned suitor."

"Oh, so? You mean she and that guy. . . ."

"Don't have any specifics on what they did together, old buddy," said Banner, absently patting Hans, or possibly Fritz, on the head. "They may have merely gone roller-discoing hand in hand, or they may have spent nights of orgiastic passion in low Chinatown dives that reeked of the seductive scent of opium. Beth had the good sense to dump the lad after a reasonably short time."

"Went with Jape Easter. . . wants to be a TV actress."

"Russ Judd isn't asking you to accept the lass's hand in marriage," reminded Banner. "All they want is somebody to lend a hand in turning out 'Poor Little Pearl' until Archie recovers."

"She's an attractive girl."

"And possibly also tan all over, I've never checked. You might ask."

A shaggy young man with a guitar case carried against his narrow chest came along the aisle. Looking back over his shoulder, he called, "Up here, Meta, we can get a front seat and stretch out."

Meta, weighted down with a cased bass fiddle, came lumbering after him.

Banner settled back in his seat, looked out the dusty window at the platform. "I believe I'll ask the syndicate for a raise," he said thoughtfully. "Did you note the number of publicity photos I took standing arm in arm with the president of the syndicate after I won the award? The smile across his pudgy face was something to behold. My contract's coming up for renewal in but two months. If their little pea brains haven't forgotten this glorious night by then, I ought to be able to hit them up for at least another five thousand per year.''

"Ah, you rich Fairfield County cartoonists," said Barney. "I've heard tales of how well you all live.''

"High on the proverbial hog," said Banner. "Why, do you realize I earn nearly as much as the plumber who came to get my rumpus-room toilet to flush again? Yes, and I only have to spend six twelve-hour days a week at the drawing board to earn it. Sunday I don't have to work at all.''

The public-address system made a sudden keening sound. A conductor with a surprisingly cultured voice announced that this was the 12:35 to New Haven and recited all the stops. A moment later bells rang, the doors whooshed shut and they started moving into the tunnel.

"You're too young to remember a radio show called 'Grand Central Station,' " said Banner.

"I am, yes.''

"Pity.'' Banner patted his award once more. "Another benefit of winning this Katzie Award will be, I think, that the price of my originals will go up. Right now a 'Dr. Judge's Family' original is worth about fifty bucks. I figure the price may soar up to at least sixty once the news of this latest achievement gets around.''

"I got the impression," Barney said, watching the dim lights of the tunnel flicker by, "from talking to Jocko Pease, that original comic art was worth a considerable amount right now."

"Some of it is," said Banner. "The sort of stuff poor Jocko lost in his fire, for instance, was worth big bucks. Take Winsor McKay, who did Little Nemo. Fans and collectors might go up to ten thousand dollars for one of his old Sunday-page originals. There's been quite a fad, too, for Herriman's Krazy Kat, although I've always thought that was the most god-awful unfunny strip I've ever seen. People have paid a thousand bucks or more for a Sunday-page original. No telling what the nitwit public will decide is of value. One of my sons, who's living with a former wife of mine, is into collecting beer cans. He doesn't drink the beer, like a sensible teenager ought, he just piles up the cans on shelves.''

The train left the tunnel, emerging amid the dingy glow of Harlem.

Barney said, "Occurs to me I don't even have any samples of Archie Judd's strip around. If I'm going to whip up some impressive samples of 'Poor Little Pearl' to show Beth and her dad, I'll need to look over proofs or tear sheets."

"I have a massive collection of tear sheets and

proofs you can borrow," offered his friend. "I've always liked Archie's work, made it a point to save it."

"Can I drop over tomorrow morning sometime to pick the stuff up?"

"Not until the cock has crowed for noon." Banner, chuckling, glanced at Barney. "You are definitely going to take a crack at the job?"

"Yeah, I am," he answered.

3

Spooky.

That was the word that occurred to Barney as he drove his eleven-year-old Volkswagen onto the dark night grounds of the Judd estate. It was a real Universal Pictures sort of night, with a hot wind howling over the high stone walls, big sooty clouds scudding across the full moon. The budding trees lining the long driveway that twisted up across the five acres of grounds looked dead and gnarled in the pale bluish moonlight. You expected to hear owls, see bats flicker across the sky.

The house itself was vast, faced with stone and cross timbers. It had a gabled roof, leaded windows, shutters, distorted-seeming spires and vanes. The light glowing behind the multi-color panes didn't look especially warm.

"Not a cozy place," decided Barney, parking his ancient VW, as instructed, in front of the long row of garages.

The white gravel crackled like all the shred-ded wheat in the world as his sneakered feet hit it. Twisting, he reached into the back seat of the car, shoving aside his tennis racket and a collection of Perrier bottles he'd been meaning to recycle, to fish out his big portfolio.

With that under his arm, he started for the heavy front door of the Judd mansion.

After about a dozen steps across the lively gravel he suddenly stopped. He'd heard a different sort of sound. Off there in the shadows between the immense house and the sprawling garages. Whistling with tongue against teeth, he bent down as if planning to tie his shoe. Setting the black portfolio carefully down, he glanced to his left at the place the noise had originated.

Scurrying commenced; someone was in there, running away now.

"Let him go," Barney advised himself as he gathered up his portfolio and stood. "For all you know old Archie also goes in for nocturnal jogging."

Although the old gent's only recreation was supposed to be bicycle riding, as had been mentioned at the N.A.G. banquet the other night. On top of which Archie Judd was ailing, which was the reason Barney was here with his samples.

The door chimes echoed dimly inside the huge old house.

Beth opened the big oaken door. She was wearing a pale yellow shirt, tan slacks. Her long hair was pulled back, tied with a single strand of ribbon. "Glad you're here." She smiled and moved back.

He stepped across the threshold into a lofty hallway. "Have you really done TV commercials?"

"Five in the past two years."

Barney nodded. "I was hoping it was only a baseless slander."

"One of them won a Mexico City Art Directors Award."

"What do they know about integrity and truth, bunch of mustached revolutionaries with bandoliers all over them," he said. "Were you aware, by the way, you had someone lurking outside?"

"What do you mean?"

"Not sure who it was, beyond your traditional dark shape," he told the girl. "I saw him prowling around next to one of the garages. When I paused to scrutinize the area, he took off in the opposite direction." Barney hesitated, watching her face, which had paled. "Have you been having trouble with prowlers? I know in my part of Westport there've been quite a few break-ins lately."

"What? Oh, prowlers, no," Beth said. "Usually they don't risk climbing over our wall. We left the front gate open because we were expecting you."

"And I let a bunch of thugs follow me in apparently. Might be worthwhile to call the police."

She shook her head. "Probably just kids," she decided. "My grandfather is something of a celebrity. Once in a while we do get curiosity seekers."

"This particular dark shape was pretty hefty to be a kid after an autographed original."

Beth took him by the arm. "Come on into the living room," she invited. "I'll fix you a drink and we can talk until my father comes down from looking after grandfather."

"But you don't want to talk anymore about this prowler?" He let her lead him into a large beam-ceilinged room.

"Even though grandfather isn't severely ill, I don't want to upset him unless we absolutely have to. If there are any further signs of someone hanging around, we'll certainly do something. Okay?"

"It's your estate." He settled onto the low sofa the girl's nod had indicated. "How many commercials was it you appeared—"

"Your drink? What would you like?"

"Perrier."

"Would you settle for club soda? Grandfather considers Perrier a needless affectation."

"Sure, club soda." He placed his portfolio on the sofa cushion next to him. "There are a lot of other careers you could pursue. Nursing, computer programming, air-conditioner repairing."

After handing him his drink, the girl sat on a bentwood rocker facing him. "You seem to have modeling mixed up with an even older profession, Barney. Actually it's a very—''

"The moral issue isn't what...oops, forgot I'm here as a job supplicant. Excuse it.'' He sipped at his club soda.

"Does that compare with Perrier?''

"Well, it might, except it's flat.''

"Darn, grandfather never puts the stoppers back on right. All the sparkle escapes.'' She gave him an apologizing smile. "Listen, if you come to work for us you can have all the contrary opinions you want. Or at least half a dozen of 'em a week anyway.''

Barney grinned. "I didn't mean to sound like Uncle Tom showing his résumé to Simon What's-his-name,'' he said. "I tend to get dangerously overzealous when I discuss modeling as a way of life.''

Beth snapped her fingers. "Darn it, I should have remembered. Ty told me about your wife...was it a divorce or a separation?''

"A heartrending agony from the way I've been acting, I guess. What it is is a legal separation that'll bloom into a divorce.''

"Do you care to talk about her?''

"Nope,'' he answered. "Well, yes, actually. Except I won't. How's your grandfather feeling?''

"Not much better.''

"Meaning you're still looking for a part-time ghost?''

"Sure, we wouldn't have had you come over to show your samples tonight if we weren't serious, Barney," Beth assured him. "There is definitely a job here, for the next few weeks at least."

Absently unlacing his portfolio, he said, "You have a really spooky estate here. Has that ever occurred to you?"

"Many times." She leaned, rubbed at her ankle. "My mother died when I was seven. Father and I moved in here then. Almost twenty years ago. The place really scared me when I was little and then when I was away in school I came across a book by H.P. Lovecraft and a story in there really reminded—"

"One goddamn bourbon and soda ain't going to kill me!" A loud, quavery voice had sounded suddenly from elsewhere in the big old house.

Another voice, most likely that of Russell Judd, said something soothing, and not quite audible, in turn.

"That nitwit quack can stuff his advice up his fanny! I'm going to have my drink."

Beth cleared her throat. "Grandfather isn't adjusting perfectly to his illness."

Barney didn't reply.

Footsteps sounded in the hall and then Russell Judd appeared, smiling uneasily. "Very good to see you again, Mr. Kains." He offered his damp hand, glancing across at his daughter. "You heard?"

"Even if I weren't attuned by this time to hear, I'd have heard." She got up to cross to the ornate liquor cabinet. "Might as well take it up to him."

"But Dr. Emerson told us distinctly not—"

"I'll come down there and pee on the company if I don't get that drink damn quick!" threatened Archie Judd from another room of the mansion.

"It's not actually senility my father's suffering from," Judd explained as he joined Beth in front of the array of bottles. "Just stubbornness, Mr. Kains, and he's had that all of his life."

Barney said, "Well, artists tend to—"

"Let's have that goddamn drink!"

"He means well, Bethany." Judd hurried toward the doorway with a drink. "I'll be back very shortly to look at the samples you've—"

"Going to count to ten!" boomed the old cartoonist's voice.

Judd left, nearly on the run.

Beth said, "Grandfather does have his nice moments."

"At the drawing board, anyway."

"You like the way he draws?"

"I didn't pay all that much attention until a few days ago," admitted Barney. "Now—and this isn't a con—when I started going over all the proofs of 'Poor Little Pearl' that Ty loaned me, I found myself really admiring his stuff.

Old-fashioned, sure, but very effective. And the story lines really make you care about that miserable little orphan girl and her bedraggled cat.''

"I suppose." Beth had decided to fix a martini for herself. "I like 'Peanuts' and 'Doonesbury' much better. Although growing up in an artistic family may have knocked my perceptions a bit cockeyed. What are your parents?''

"Neither cockeyed nor artists," he replied. "My father was an insurance salesman and my mother taught grade school most of her life. That was out in California and they're both dead now.''

"I'm sorry.''

"I have mixed feelings, especially about my dad.''

"Only child?''

"Yep.''

"Me, too." She smiled at him across the top of her glass. "That gives us a basis, I think, for a permanent friendship.''

"At least one that'll last as long as I ghost 'Pearl' for you. If I do.''

"You're pretty guarded, Barney.''

"Part of the only-child syndrome.''

"Not in my case, I tend to trust almost—''

A loud crash from upstairs in the mansion, glass broke.

Barney popped to his feet. "Trouble?''

"Sit," advised the dark-haired girl. "It's only

grandfather throwing something at my dad. Most of the time he's really quite nice and even tempered. When he's sick, which isn't often, he can be an ogre.''

"The Human Beast is like that. One minute he's a mild-mannered male model in a fashionable Manhattan—''

"Bourbon and soda isn't supposed to be all soda pop, Russ! Did that skinny little Betsy mix this one?''

After a silent moment Judd reappeared in the living room. "I'll mix one more and then. . .'' he said, lips barely parted. "You must forgive us, Mr. Kains. Bethany can assure you this isn't S.O.P. around the Judd household.''

"She has, yes.''

When Judd left them again, the girl said, "Why don't I take a look at your samples while dad is playing artful dodger with grandfather?''

"Fine by me.'' He flipped the portfolio open, spread out the four sample daily "Poor Little Pearl'' strips he'd whipped up since meeting Beth and her father at the Newspaper Artists Guild banquet. "The continuity I cooked up myself, trying to get in all the main characters. Pearl herself, Muffin the cat, Uncle Goodworx, Mrs. Narsty, Goombah the Wizard and so on.''

Beth knelt before the yawning portfolio. "Darn,'' she said, head bobbing. "Darn.''

"Could you translate that into layman's terms?''

Laughing, she stood. "You're really damn good." A touch of surprise lingered in her voice. "You've got the thing down just about perfect. Darn."

"That disappoints you?"

"In spite of Ty's glowing recommendation of you, I wasn't anticipating your being this good at all," she said, sipping at her martini. "The darn is just my way of chiding myself for not having more faith. I was expecting that a comic-book artist, somebody who drew . . . what is the name of your comic-book thing? About the guy who gets all blue and hairy and beats up people?"

"That's the exact name of it. *The Guy Who Gets All Blue and Hairy and Beats Up People Comics*. It'll look damn good on the screen, too, if we ever get a movie nibble."

"Human Beast, I remember now, and you just mentioned him during grandfather's tantrum." She poked at the tiny onion in her glass. "Somehow you don't expect someone who spends his days drawing the Human Beast to be able to draw anything much good."

Barney inquired, "Is this supposed to be a test of my temper, miss? You make snide digs about my talent, or lack thereof, and I go berserk, turn all hairy and blue, throw my drink at you and stomp out into the night?"

"I'm sorry, really." She came nearer, touched at his arm. "I'm only trying to be honest. Probably that does sound like nastiness at times."

He liked the nearness of the girl. "My fault for being touchy. After a couple years with Maximus Comics, Inc., I tend not to trust anybody I work for."

Patting his arm she backed off. "You can trust us, Barney," she said softly. "And we really won't be anywhere near as nasty as I hear some of the people up at Maximus are."

He said, "Publishing so many magazines about monsters has taken its toll on them."

Russell Judd returned, shoulders slouched. "I think Archie is settled for the night. He sends his best wishes, Mr. Kains."

"So I heard."

"You'll get to like him. Most of the time he's—"

"Dad, I already gave Barney the spiel," Beth cut in. "And you can quit calling him Mr. Kains and switch to Barney."

"Oh?"

"Because he's going to be working for us," she announced.

4

JUAN TEXACO HAD DESERTED his drawing board
to gaze out the narrow office's lone window
down at Madison Avenue, aided by an ancient
pair of binoculars.

Standing in the doorway, portfolio under his
arm, Barney watched his friend for a moment
before saying, "I'm here to check out com-
plaints about a peeping Tom."

"Ah, the ghost who walks." Texaco, lowering
the green-tinted glasses, turned to grin at him.
"I suspected you were in with our esteemed
managing editor, since Carlotsky's got a different scream of rage for each of us in the flock.
Mine is pitched to shatter crystal goblets, yours
could be used to guide ocean liners in the fog.
Didn't he like the latest Human Beast epic?"

"Matter of fact, he loved it, suggesting only
that I add a wee bit more saliva drooling out of
each lobsterman before inking." Coming into
the office, Barney dropped his portfolio on the
other, unoccupied, drawing board. "Where's
Warloff today?"

"Asleep in the john I think." Texaco was back to surveying the sunny afternoon street far below. "It's tough to be an old-timer in this business, without the aid of artificial stimulants. Warloff's the only chap off the Bowery I've ever actually seen drink muscatel. So what's Carlotsky ranting over?"

"He seems to have heard I'm going to do some work on 'Poor Little Pearl.'"

"I heard a similar rumor. True?"

Tapping his portfolio, Barney replied, "I'll be turning in six dailies and two Sundays to the Judds tonight. Brought 'em along so you can give me an opinion."

"Put in more spittle," suggested the curly-haired cartoonist. "Wow, there is a girl who is a dead ringer for Gail Russell. Oh, but it looks like she's bent on turning tricks. Can such a sweet and angelic face hide—"

"Want to look at this junk? I want to slink out of Maximus before Carlotsky thinks of some new indignity to try on me."

"Did he threaten you with Peter Pupp?"

"Not as yet."

"Imagine a sword of Damocles shaped like Peter Pupp." Clinking his binoculars down atop a battered green filing cabinet, Texaco rubbed his palms together. "Come, young sir, let us see these samples. Then I'll tell you whether you have a future in penal servitude or not."

Untying the black portfolio, Barney extracted

six 'Pearl' daily originals and arranged them on Warloff's vacant drawing board. "I think I've pretty much got Archie Judd's style down."

"Are you boasting or lamenting?" Hands locked behind his back, Texaco bent over the display of strips. "I especially love Judd's dialogue. Yep, there's Pearl herself exclaiming, 'Jimmyjams!' just as she's done for a full half century. Ah, and here we have her faithful pussycat Muffin howling out, 'Yarp!' Did you ever encounter a real feline who spoke thusly? Yarp? What self-respecting cat would say that? No, they use such phrases as 'Rowr,' or—"

"No good, huh?" Barney started to gather the drawings up.

Texaco stayed his hand. "What do you want to hear, old friend?" he inquired, looking up at him. "Sure, you've done a perfect job of aping the old coot's style, even improved on it in many subtle ways. If I congratulate you, though, it's sort of like complimenting somebody for being a spitting image of Ernest Borgnine. What do you think about the work?"

"I think I can use the extra six hundred bucks a week I'm going to make for doing this."

"That's perfectly rational."

"I also think Beth Judd is damn nice, for a would-be model."

"Another point in your favor." Texaco, with a skating motion, returned to his window. "This morning, whilst Warloff was enjoying the first of a series of short naps, I actually spotted a lass down below who was an exact and well-nigh perfect copy of Eleanor Powell. Nifty legs and all.''

Barney slipped the ''Pearl'' drawings away. ''You're implying I ought to be doing better things,'' he said. ''That's the kind of message Tawny was continually—''

''Damnation! I just lost fifty centavos.'' Shrugging, Texaco grabbed up his binoculars. ''I had bet myself that you, dazzled by your new position as a big-time newspaper-strip artist and already well on the way to plummeting head over heels in love with darling Bethany, would actually be able to spend a full five minutes in my humble anchorite's cell without mentioning that ex-mate of yours. But no.''

''Only once so far,'' said Barney. ''That's, you have to admit, a hell of an improvement over two months ago.''

''To get rid of an addiction like yours, you have to go absolutely cold turkey.''

''You know, I saw her on the train coming in from Westport today.''

Texaco tapped the glasses against his chin. ''In the flesh?''

''No, no, one of her damn ad posters,'' he answered. ''For Ms. Health cigarettes. She was coming out of the surf in South America somewhere and looking incredibly.... Don't know why they let them post those things in the no-smoking cars.''

''Part of a vast international conspiracy, designed to drive conservative middle-aged men mad with lust while at the same time slipping their spouses a dose of terminal lung cancer.'' Texaco, feet dragging, returned himself to sit at his slanted drawing board. ''Wonder if I can have this Nazi lizardman exclaim, 'Jimmyjams!' when Flaming Death sets him afire.''

''Try 'Yarp!' ''

''No, I'm going to have a bigger balloon than that to fill,'' said Texaco. ''Sometimes I wish I weren't the multiple threat I am, and didn't have to pencil, ink, letter and script this *merde*.''

Barney sat in Warloff's chair. ''Did you ever meet Archie Judd?''

''A few times. At one of the N.A.G. doings a couple years back, and once at a picnic given by the photoengravers of Manhattan or some such group. He's a crusty old bird, if memory serves. How's he strike you?''

''Well, I haven't actually met him as yet,'' explained Barney. ''He's been too sick.''

''Won't you tonight, when you lay all this artwork on the wide-eyed Judd clan?''

''Possibly. So far, the two evenings I've called at the mansion, he was up in bed. I have heard him a lot, though. Yelling and thumping.''

"What's he thump?"

"The floor. With his cane."

"That's a nice old curmudgeon touch." Texaco selected a pencil from the tin cup full of them on his low filing cabinet. "Did you ever happen to see anyone break a Nazi lizardman's neck with a karate chop? My swipe file is sadly lacking in such depictions."

"You do it like this." Standing, Barney chopped at the air. "I was pretty good at karate, back in college."

"Do it once more, in slow motion, please. I'll capture it with my immortal pencil." Hunching, Texaco began roughing in the figure of his hero.

Barney repeated the action. "Draw fast, I don't like the idea of working as a model."

"The Judds are paying you six bills per week?"

"Yeah."

"Where is all the big money I hear can be earned in the syndicate vineyards? Hell's fire, I can do thrice that a week if I wasn't continually being distracted by fleshly temptations."

"An extra six hundred a week right now is dandy with me. I don't want to screw the situation up by asking for more."

Leaning back, tickling his ear with the eraser end of his pencil, Texaco said, "They have a word for folks who sell their talents for money, amigo. It escapes me at the moment."

"Commercial artist is the term you're groping for," said Barney. Retrieving his portfolio, he eased for the door. "I better depart, I'm aiming for the 4:05."

"Ah, the life of the dashing commuter. We wetbacks up in Brooklyn Heights sure envy you, squire," Texaco said. "Well, good luck with your newfound fortune. I think maybe you're moving up out of the depths of despair."

"A few rungs anyway," Barney said.

THE LATE-AFTERNOON SUN was shining down on Westport. After parking his aging Volkswagen beside the mighty Saugatuck River, acing out a silver-haired matron in a week-old Mercedes, Barney went hurrying from the crowded riverside parking area and around to Main Street. While driving up from the train station, he'd suddenly decided he'd like a bottle of Dr. Brown's Cream Soda, as a switch from his usual Perrier. The place for that was Oscar's deli. They closed at six, or even earlier if the mood hit them.

He didn't pay attention to the guy sitting in one of the deck chairs scattered in front of Oscar's. Not until he came looming up to block Barney's entrance.

"You're that son of a bitch," said the large blond young man. He was wide, had newscaster's hair.

"Try to be more specific." Barney took a step back and recognized the roadblock. "Jape Easter."

"You're not even a cartoonist," accused Easter.

"Right, I'm actually the last of the French Impressionists," he said. "Now we have that cleared up, move on out of—"

"I understand," said Easter, placing a palm on Barney's chest, "you've been hanging around Beth."

Immediately inside the blocked doorway two chunky teenage girls in fifty-dollar jeans were at the cash register buying a half-dozen napoleons and a six-pack of Dr. Brown. The scents of corned beef, rye bread, mustard and pastry came wafting out of the long narrow deli.

Barney's left eye narrowed slightly. "Look, Easter, we both live hereabouts," he said evenly, "but so far we haven't had anything to do with each other. I'd really like to keep it that way. Take your hand off me now."

After a few seconds the larger man obliged. "Okay for now, Kains," he said. "But it's not too smart to hang around the Judd place. Wisest to drop the whole business. You know?"

"Thanks for the advice. Always nice to get tips from fellow artists." He edged around the hulking cartoonist, resisting the impulse to give him an elbow in the ribs, and pushed on into Oscar's.

"I'm not kidding," said Easter at his back.

Barney bought an entire six-pack of cream soda.

5

BETH CROSSED THE LARGE STUDIO. After hesitating a second, she put her arms around Barney and kissed him on the cheek. "You're wonderful," she said.

"As a person or as an artist?"

Smiling, the girl retreated a few feet. "Right now I was referring mostly to this first week of 'Pearl' strips you've done." She toyed with the collar of the plaid shirt she was wearing under her dark green pullover. "Although you might turn out to be a wonderful person, too. We'll see."

Barney walked to the big worktable where his drawings were spread out. "I had a little trouble with Goombah's turban," he said, pointing at one of the Sunday-page drawings. "Your grandfather has it wound the wrong way."

"I know, we get at least a dozen letters a year about that."

Rubbing his fingertips across the small blank square he'd left in the corner of the last panel, he asked, "You want me to go up with you when you get your grandfather to sign these? I'd like to—''

"We want you to meet grandfather, too,'' Beth said, glancing up at the slanting skylight. The night sky was clear, rich with stars. "Thing is, he really isn't any better at all. Dr. Emerson says there's nothing to worry about...yet. Visitors I'm afraid would excite him, which we can't have.''

"Okay, I don't want to endanger his health.'' Leaving the worktable, he roamed the old man's studio.

The walls were thick with framed photos and drawings, souvenirs of Archie Judd's nearly fifty years in the limelight.

"That's Greta Garbo he's shaking hands with,'' said Beth, watching him.

"This one in the cloche hat?'' He realized it was indeed Garbo standing next to the stocky freckled man who was the Archie Judd of several decades ago.

"Grandfather worked out in Hollywood for a few years in the early thirties. They made two 'Pearl' movies back then.''

"I didn't know that.''

"Starring someone named Mitzi Green as Pearl. I've never seen them, grandfather never got a print and they don't show up on TV.''

"There's a new movie in the works, isn't there?''

She seated herself on a rattan sofa. "We hope

so," Beth answered. "A movie outfit's taken an option on the musical. If that's a success, then there'll definitely be a film. It really seems as though the Judd fortunes are going to take a great leap forward. Grandfather's remaining years should be quite comfortable."

"My impression is the Judds have already done fairly well," he said. "Quite a few cartoonists I know, even in affluent Fairfield County here, don't live exactly on this scale."

"I didn't mean to poor-mouth. Grandfather's been very successful most of his life," she said. " 'Pearl' still appears in more than five hundred papers in this country, nearly as many in Europe and South America. Only country we really do badly in is Japan."

"Could be they don't take kindly to waifs over there." Barney couldn't concentrate on the browning photographs of long-gone stars and graphic artists or on the impressive framed originals by many of his boyhood idols. He kept studying instead the slim girl on the sofa.

"Something wrong?" She smoothed her tweed skirt. "You seem to be staring at me in an odd way, as though I'd suddenly materialized before you."

"Actually I've been ogling you," he admitted as he sat in a white wicker chair to face her. "You really are . . . petite."

"Is that good?"

"In your case, yes."

"I imagined you'd be more inclined toward girls who're . . . immense."

"My former wife was tall," he acknowledged, watching his foot tap on the mat rug.

"She's very pretty."

"So all the polls indicate."

Beth smiled quietly. "In a way, Barney, you and I have similar problems. I've always lived in the shadow of 'Poor Little Pearl,' you've been going around for years as a sort of footnote to Tawny Kains."

"Actually we were married less than three years," he said.

"That's long enough for it to get uncomfortable. Are you still officially married to her?"

"As I told you before we're legally separated, heading for a permanent split."

"You sound unhappy about that."

"I . . . I'm not certain anymore if I am or not." He raised his head, eyes meeting hers.

"Would you—"

A loud thumping began elsewhere in the house.

"Let me see his damn hen scratches," Archie Judd's voice demanded. "I'll decide if they're up to snuff."

"He really liked your samples," Beth quickly said. "This time of night he's usually cranky."

Cranky? Whacking his kin with a cudgel, throwing crockery around his sickroom. That transcended Barney's idea of cranky. To him cranky seldom went much further than your wife telling you she had a headache and wanted to go to bed early.

"Suppose," he asked the girl, "your grandfather doesn't like this first batch I'm turning in?"

"Oh, he'll like everything."

"That other garbage you showed me was stiffer than a dog's hind leg," hollered the old cartoonist upstairs. "I bet he's just another mooncalf who's here to tomcat after skinny little Bethany."

Beth coughed. "I read, if that's the proper word, a stack of back issues of your Human Beast comic book," she said. "You do quite a nice job on that. I'm sorry I—"

"What was that clattering?"

"Oh, grandfather likes to fling his bedpan when he's in certain moods," she said. "You tend to undervalue your own work, don't you?"

"The comic-book stuff maybe. Sometimes I try to convince myself I'm only slumming," he answered.

"I'd like to see your other work, the serious material."

"Sure, some rainy night we can go through my sample books."

Beth shook her head. "I really am serious about—"

"Right now! Don't you know what right now means?"

"I think your grandfather wants to see my drawings." Barney left his chair. "I can take them up to—"

"No, don't do that." she cut off his advance to the worktable. "It really isn't safe to go barging in there now. My father will come. . . . Oh, hi, dad. I was trying to convince Barney that grandfather isn't a completely goofy monster."

"He's not completely goofy, no." Russell Judd came into the studio. "I really hope some night you'll drop in and not witness a family squabble, Barney."

"Actually they brighten up my otherwise lonely bachelor existence."

"The more I repeat this the less you're going to believe it," said Judd, "but my father is really a very kind and gentle man. This illness has turned him, only temporarily I hope, into a real burden. My . . . these are wonderful."

"I told him exactly the same thing." Beth joined her father beside the spread-out comic strips Barney had drawn. "Look how perfectly he's got Pearl already. Muffin looks great there where he's scratching at Mrs. Narsty."

Judd glanced up to nod at Barney. "These are even better than the samples."

"The more I do it, the easier the job becomes. If I keep at it a couple more weeks, you should see—"

"We'll need at least three more weeks' work," said Judd. "Even if Archie starts rallying, it's going to be a while before he can safely return to the drawing board." Picking up one of the Sunday pages, he held it out at arm's length. "That's a splendid long shot of the orphanage. Very nice."

"Thanks."

Beth moved closer to Barney, took hold of his arm. "You've impressed two out of three Judds."

Her father gathered the six dailies into a pile, placed them atop the two Sundays and tucked the whole collection under his arm. "I'm sure Archie'll love these," he said. "Even so, I won't write your week's check for you until he's signed all of them."

"Is he up to that?"

Moving out the door, Judd said, "He insists he is."

When he was gone, Beth said, "Even after grandfather is up and around again, we'll still have work for you. Dad and I have been trying to convince him we need someone to do the Sunday page all the time. That would take an awful lot of the pressure off him. There'll probably be quite a few subsidiary drawings to do, too, if the musical and the TV series really get going. Would you be interested?"

Barney was standing with his head tilted to the right. "Excuse me, I was listening for a reaction from above," he said. "Would six dailies being flung across a bedroom make enough noise to be heard down here in the studio? Ripping them to shreds I think I could definitely hear.''

Beth laughed. ''We sure haven't made a favorable impression on you,'' she said. ''You must think we're all as spooky as this old house. With a skeleton in every closet and a crazed old aunt chained in the attic.''

''Do you? Her I'd love to get a look at.''

''Unfortunately, we're a very quiet, sober and possibly dull lot, Barney.''

Judd returned with the drawings under his opposite arm. ''My father was charmed by your work.''

''I think he was initially a bit miffed to see someone imitating his style so well.'' He laid the drawings out on the worktable. ''Beth, you better put the syndicate copyright notices on these.''

''Wish they were copyrighted by Archie Judd.'' She picked up a book of small gummed labels.

Barney looked over the strips he'd ghosted. Scratched on each, in the boxes he'd left for that purpose, was the familiar Archie Judd signature. Done all in uppercase letters with an exaggerated dot over the *I*.

''Well, it's official now,'' he said, mostly to himself, ''I'm a ghost.''

6

HE WAS SEATED at the drawing board, watching a squirrel raid his bird feeder when the phone rang. Turning away from the gray morning outside, Barney answered. "Hello?"

"A word of warning," shouted Texaco at the other end.

"Hey, why so loud?"

"Forgive me, amigo. I think my last encounter with Carlotsky shattered my eardrums, thus I'm having a tough time judging decibel levels."

Barney rested his foot on a strut of the board frame. "What did you want to warn me about?"

"Let me do a little preambling first," said the cartoonist in a lowered voice. "Seems Warloff, who's been doing Peter Pupp in his inimitable somnambulistic style, has had another of his seizures. In fact, he had it right here in our portion of the Maximus bull pen."

"You mean he's in a coma?"

"No, no, with Warloff dozing is his natural state, when he's sick he gets hyperactive," explained Texaco. "This morning he commenced having hallucinations just after the coffee wagon departed. Claimed all the characters he's drawn in comic books since his debut as a fuzz-faced youth back in 1943 had come back to haunt him. He wanted me to help fend off an attack force that included Pyroman, the Fighting Yank, the Purple Zombie, the Sniper, Mr. E. Airmale and Posty, Subzero Man, the Blue Bolt, the Gay Ghost and Bozo the Robot. It was a sad, albeit nostalgic—"

"They carted the poor bastard off?"

"He was in Bellevue at last report."

"So Carlotsky's going to need somebody to take over on Peter Pupp maybe?"

"I fear so. I was able to talk my way out of the chore, but you may not be so lucky."

"Thanks for the warning," said Barney. "I'll avoid the phone for a while. Maybe by tomorrow Warloff will be recovered."

"A guy who thinks the Star Spangled Kid and Stripsey are goosing him may not rally all that fast."

"We can only hope. If they collect for a get-well gift, put me down for a buck."

Texaco asked, "How's the nationally syndicated part of your life going?"

"I'm due to turn in my third week of dailies tonight."

"Has Archie Judd dandled you on his knee as yet?"

"Actually, Texaco, I still haven't met him. Seems he's got some kind of chest ailment on top of the flu."

"Boy, if it's not muscatel that gets you, it's germs. Hardly seems worth getting old for," observed Texaco.

"I've been wondering if maybe old Archie isn't in a lot worse shape than they're letting on."

"Aw, look on the bright side," said Texaco. "It's more likely he's simply taken a deep and abiding loathing to you, based entirely on looking at your drawings. When you're not around he probably has tons of guests flocking up to his bedchambers."

"Tell you somebody who does loathe me."

"Not the sweet and gentle Beth?"

"No, that jerk I had the rumpus with back at the N.A.G. banquet."

"James Perry Easter, alias J.P. Easter, also known as Jape Easter. That the jerk you mean?"

"The same," answered Barney. "I've had a couple run-ins with him in Westport lately. Macho stuff, where he glowers at me like Robert Conrad in those battery commercials."

"That's what you get for dwelling in that artists' colony out there, amigo," said his friend. "Artists are a notoriously quarrelsome lot. By the way, did it ever occur to you how much Beth resembles that 1930s screen beauty Paulette Goddard?"

"Never did, no."

"Have you and Jape exchanged punches?"

"Not yet, though maybe soon," Barney said. "Couple nights ago somebody phoned me at 3:00 A.M. I went stumbling out of bed to the phone. Guy on the other end just whispered, 'Bastard,' and hung up."

"You sure it wasn't simply the operator delivering a singing telegram from Carlotsky?"

"Not sure who it was, although Jape Easter has a top spot on my suspect list. I don't like to be tangled up with cranks."

Texaco laughed. "You should've thought of that before signing on with Maximus."

"Not that kind of crank."

"Have you mentioned Jape's assaults to Beth?"

"Don't want to do that," he said. "Especially since I found out she used to date the guy."

"No accounting for taste," sighed Texaco. "Well, back to the old drawing board. Let's have lunch sometime."

"It's a date." After hanging up, Barney took the phone off the hook.

To him Peter Pupp was like the fatal glass of beer, the one step he was afraid would doom him forever to a life in the comic-book business. Peter Pupp, his cross-eyed sidekick Silly Spaniel, his sweetheart Penny Pooch.

"God, imagine being haunted by them in my old age." He left his board.

A cold wind was whooshing down through the chimney, scattering the ashes of his collection of magazine pictures of Tawny. Could be he really was making progress, since he'd been able to burn all those last night without shedding a tear or grabbing them back off the flames.

He picked *TV Guide* from the sofa. "Let's see what the noon movie is. *Way of a Gaucho* with Rory Calhoun. Yeah, that's right, this is Rory Calhoun Week. Will Rory Calhoun in *Way of a Gaucho* cheer me up or push me over the edge?"

Bending, he clicked on the small color set.

". . . back right after these messages to watch the lovely Tawny Kains show us what sort of skimpy and scandalous bikinis we can expect to see on our beaches come summer."

"No, nope!" He lunged, unplugged the set and carried it to a dark corner of the living room, where he placed it with its face to the wall.

Watching his lost wife parade by in skimpy and scandalous swimsuits would do him no good at all.

"A drive," he decided. "Yeah, I'll take a drive."

A light rain started to fall as he crossed to where his old Volkswagen sat huddled in its drafty garage.

THE RAIN WAS COMING HEAVIER when Barney drove onto the grounds of the Judd estate. Everything looked just as gloomy, on this his first daytime visit, as it did in the dead of night. Yet he felt cheerful; the idea of an extra visit with Beth caused that. He hadn't phoned, figuring simply to drop by and maybe ask the girl if she'd like to have lunch. Not at Mario's or the Inkwell or Porky Manero's, places where artists and cartoonists were known to hang out; but someplace a lot more cozy and quiet. The sort of restaurant he'd never been able to talk Tawny into going to.

Barney parked in his usual spot in front of the row of garages. The rain was hitting at the tiled gables of the mansion, water was gurgling down through green-stained copper drainpipes. Turning up the collar of his Windbreaker, he started a dash from his car toward the front entrance of the vast house.

Something distracted him.

A door slammed around back somewhere, heavy feet went running across the gravel.

"Damn, is that the phantom autograph hound again?" He ducked into the alley between mansion and garages.

Framed at the other distant end was a dark figure. Someone bundled in a black slicker and hat—the kind of gear everybody wore in whaling movies—was galloping off in the direction of the woods behind the house.

Barney kicked up his pace, splashing across muddy ground and through brownish puddles. White sneakers, he realized, were probably not the best footwear for this sort of work.

The other man was up among the maples and white birches, a huge lump rolling along through the crosshatch of trunks and branches.

A pain started in Barney's calf, went shooting up his leg until it slammed into his groin. Not the best time for a pulled muscle.

Grimacing, he kept slogging along.

The hard rain had no trouble getting down through the branches and new leaves. It smacked at Barney as he ran through the upward slanting woodland.

"Where the hell is he?"

He could hear the crackling of the man's retreat, but he'd lost sight of the black-coated figure.

Barney was breathing through his mouth, his throat dry. A snaking root, unnoticed until too late, hooked its loop around his left foot. He fell forward, slamming into the mossy ground. Water, mud and a rich compost of last autumn's leaves splashed up all around him.

"Deft," he told himself as he pushed up off the soggy ground. "Very deft."

He stood for a moment and listened. There was no sound of the other runner. "Better see if everybody's okay at the house."

He trudged downhill through the rainswept

woods, brushing at the splotches of mud on his clothes with some wadded-up tissues from his pocket.

No one answered when he pushed at the bell next to the back door. A series of knocks, accompanied with a call of, "Anybody home?" also produced nothing.

With a damp shrug he tried the knob. The door opened and he stepped across into a large laundry room. A wicker basket filled with filmy white lingerie rested atop the pale blue dryer beside a huge box of detergent with comic-book lettering on its front.

Barney tugged off his wet sneakers, left them on the prickly mat just inside the door.

"Beth!" He moved out of the laundry room and into a shadowy yellow corridor. "Beth? Mr. Judd?"

Only silence.

Had that guy in the whaler outfit been carrying anything? Loot or a weapon? He could have burgled the house, knocked out Beth and the others.

No, he didn't have anything in his hands.

Still he might have been an escaped madman. He may not have taken anything, just come to strangle everyone.

"Beth? Mr. Judd?"

He refrained from calling Archie Judd's name, not wanting to annoy the old man.

"Beth? Anybody here?"

Pushing through a doorway, he found himself in the front hall.

The drumming of the rain was enlarged here, it filled the place.

No one was in the living room, dead or alive. There was not a trace of a struggle. Rain was hitting at the charred logs in the big fireplace.

There was a copy of last month's issue of *Human Beast Comics* on the coffee table.

"Flattering." He left.

The studio was empty, too. So proved to be all the other first-floor rooms.

After a while he no longer expected to find anything. Barney had begun to get the feeling he was absolutely alone in the big old house.

"But then where's Archie?"

Had the old man grown worse, been rushed to Norwalk Hospital?

That would explain where Beth and her father were. Although it didn't provide any answers about the guy who'd gone batting out of here when he'd heard Barney's VW come rattling up.

In the hallway again he hesitated at the foot of the wide curving staircase leading up to the second floor of the mansion.

Maybe he'd already screwed up his ghosting job by doing what amounted to housebreaking. Still, he had to make sure they were all okay. Beth especially.

"It's Barney Kains," he called upstairs

through cupped hands. "Your assistant, Archie. I'm coming up."

The flowered runner was thickly padded. His stockinged feet sank into the steps. Hell of a lot of steps. He went climbing up and up, tensed and ready to make a move or an apology.

Windows on the landing were of stained glass, leaded. The rain was trickling down across the colored panes.

"Archie? Mr. Judd? Is everything all right up here? Reason I ask, I bumped into a burglar as I came in." He was shouting this as he entered the dim hallway. "Reason I dropped in, it has nothing to do with the strip. More a social call."

The first door on his left was partially open. He got a glimpse of a large four-poster, a dark rug, draped windows, and walls covered with framed drawings and photos.

This had to be Archie Judd's bedroom.

Barney pulled the door, gingerly, all the way open. "Excuse my . . . ."

There was no one in the bed. It was neatly made, covered with a patchwork quilt.

If they'd rushed the old man off to the hospital, nobody would have stopped to make the bed.

On the wall behind the bed were framed pictures and drawings similar to the mix downstairs in the old cartoonist's studio.

"To the one an' only Arch! From his pal Sidney Smith!" Barney read from a colored

drawing of a chinless man he suspected must be
Andy Gump. "Lots of love, Archie. Your sweetheart, Ann Sheridan." Cartoonists had a more
colorful life in those days. Yeah, that must be
Jean Harlow up there next to Toots and Casper,
and that other picture of the girl hugging Archie. . . I ought to have Texaco here to identify
all these women.

Sitting on a heavy mahogany bedside table
was an expensive cassette recorder-player. It
was, he discovered when he went around the
other side of the four-poster, rigged up to a
stereo receiver. One of the speakers was beside
the bed, the other was, for some reason, placed
next to the doorway and aimed outward.

Leaning, narrowing his eyes, he determined
there was a cassette on the machine, ready to
play.

Jean Harlow was staring down at him.

Barney reached out, full of curiosity, pushed
down the play switch.

"Where the heck's that toddy?" boomed Archie Judd's voice out of the speakers. "Bring it
quick or there'll be trouble!"

7

"WHERE THE HECK'S THAT TODDY?" called Archie Judd's voice. "Bring it quick or there'll be trouble!"

Eyes on Beth's face, Barney remarked, "Your grandfather sounds somewhat better tonight."

"He does seem to be bitching in healthier tones tonight, doesn't he?" She went to the living-room doorway. "Want me to fix that, dad?"

From the kitchen Judd replied, "No, I'm already doing it, dear."

Is her father really back there? Or has she got Russell Judd prerecorded, too.

"Those two latest Sunday pages look great." The girl perched on the arm of the sofa near him.

"Thanks." He glanced away from her. "Tried to phone you this afternoon."

"Dad and I had to go down to the bank," Beth explained. "One of those situations where they insisted we both had to sign some papers. The vice-president who'd told us that came back late from a very wet lunch and the whole business took much longer than it should've. Was there some problem?"

"Nothing to do with the strip," he said. "I only wanted to talk to you."

"About what?"

He smiled. "Do you have a list of categories I can pick from?"

"I see, you meant you just wanted to talk."

"The way friends and associates sometimes do, yeah." He shifted on the sofa. "When you and your father go out, who looks after Archie?"

Beth left the arm of the sofa and went over to rearrange some books on the built-in shelves near the fireplace. "Usually we get a relatively reliable teenage girl from down the road, Terri Wormser. Today, though, she's got the flu, too, but her mother was nice enough to come in her place."

"Very neighborly."

Beth eyed him over her shoulder. "There's an odd tone in your voice," she said. "Something wrong?"

"Damp weather makes me sound this way, nothing to worry about. I wonder why Ms. Wormser didn't answer the phone when I called."

"Usually we turn it down when grandfather's napping."

He locked his hands over one knee. "For a

moment there this afternoon I thought maybe Archie'd gotten worse.''

"Nice of you to worry, but he's not.'' She moved a book to a lower shelf. "He's not much better either, though. Looks like we'll have to keep on asking you to help out for a few more weeks.''

Nodding, he said, "You know, I don't even have a doctor, not a G.P. Been thinking I ought to have a physical, just to see what shape I'm really in. What's your doctor's name?''

"Dr. Emerson, but he really specializes in older people.''

"Is that the guy who has an office over in Norwalk?''

"No, he's in Westport, in that crazy office complex on Route 33 that everybody calls Fort Apache.''

"He won't touch anyone under seventy?''

She laughed. "He prefers older patients, but I suppose you could see him. What do you think is wrong with you?''

"Nothing really. It's only that I've been reading about preventive medicine and—''

"Those new Sunday pages look fine, Barney.'' Judd, brushing at his thinning hair, came into the living room. "We got the proofs of your first week of dailies in today. Has Beth shown them to you?''

"I forgot.'' She eased toward the doorway. "I'll fetch them.''

Barney said, "Archie's about the same, huh?"

"I'm afraid so," answered Judd. "Dr. Emerson says it's going to be a very slow recovery."

"He sounded pretty hale and hearty calling for his toddy."

"This bug hasn't quite robbed him of his ability to holler when he wants something."

What the hell was going on here in this mansion? They were both lying to him, Beth especially. Where was Archie Judd? Barney knew if he went up to that bedroom now, the old cartoonist still wouldn't be there.

"They look quite handsome." Beth held up a sheet of glossy paper on which six 'Poor Little Pearl' strips were printed in sequence. Independent Features Syndicate was printed large across the top of the page of proofs.

He took the sheet, studied it. "Damn, the crosshatching on the cottage broke up."

"We've been having a little trouble with I.F.S.'s new engraver," said Judd. "A delicate line will get lost now and then."

Okay, so Archie isn't up in the bedroom. Where then? "Goombah looks okay, even with his turban tied backward."

"All in all, it's a terrific job," Beth told him. "A very impressive debut."

Did they have him locked in the cellar? Maybe the old boy had gone completely bonkers. They kept him chained to the wall, fed him on table scraps.

"Joe Langendorf was quite impressed."

"The president of the syndicate knows I'm doing this?"

"We told him we were bringing in an assistant," answered Judd.

Beth added, "We're not trying to hide anything."

Except Archie. They couldn't have knocked him off, could they? Put something in one of his toddies, dragged him out under cover of darkness and buried him in the woods? It all sounded too melodramatic. And, damn it, Beth would never be a party to anything like that. He knew that. The thing was, though, Archie was not upstairs in that bedroom. Beth and her father were both, for whatever reason, trying to convince him he was.

"Real Perrier," Beth was saying. "Want a twist in it?"

He looked up from the proof sheet. "Excuse me, I was so enthralled with my own work I didn't hear you."

"We bought a six-pack of Perrier," she said. "Would you like a drink?"

"Sure, that'll be fine." There had to be an explanation for all this. He had to stop suspecting that Beth was another Lizzie Borden. He knew damn well he couldn't be in love with a murderess. Oops. In love? He hadn't intended to fall in love just yet. Not so soon after Tawny, not with another girl who had model inclinations—

"Or lime?" Beth was asking him.

He stood up, clutching at the proofs. "Lime."

No, really there must be a simple and logical explanation. Oh, really, Mr. Spock, and what the hell is it? You ran that damn tape back to the spot it'd been set on so they wouldn't know you'd played it. You slipped out of there this afternoon, making sure all traces of your visit were cleaned up. And what did they do? They went right ahead and used the tape, used it to try and con you. You are supposed to believe Archie Judd is up there right now being his usual curmudgeonly self. He isn't up there, however, which you know damn well. He probably hasn't ever been up there, not from the first night you wandered into this mess. The question, then, is if he's not—

"Keep this set if you'd like," Judd was telling him.

Blinking, Barney looked again at the proofs. "Thanks, that'll be helpful," he said. "Maybe I'll even start a scrapbook. Even if it's only going to run a few pages."

"You'll be doing enough work for us to fill up a book, don't worry," said Judd.

Barney stayed in the living room another fifteen minutes with them, drinking his Perrier with a lime twist, carrying on a conversation he was only partly tuned-in on.

Beth saw him to the door when he left. As she handed him his portfolio, she stretched up and

kissed his cheek. "Thanks for helping," she
said.

Making his way through the misty night to his
old Volkswagen, he said, "Damn, I wish she
hadn't done that."

8

THE INKWELL RESTAURANT, as its name suggests, is a hangout for artists, cartoonists,
writers. A ramshackle shingled place, it hangs
out over the Saugatuck River and is within
sprinting distance of the Westport train station.
There are several wide windows, offering as-
sorted views of the narrow river and the buildings that fringe it. The walls are a patchwork of
framed drawings and improvised sketches done
directly on the peach-colored plaster. Leaning
at the bar today were Stan Drake and Leonard
Starr. They both waved at Barney as he came
in. He waved back, kept moving toward the
table in the far corner where Ty Banner was
already seated. He edged around a table where
Zarley and Joe Ferris were having lunch, probably talking over things up at the *New Yorker*.
Barney wasn't here for shoptalk.

"There's been a small change in plans, old
buddy," announced Banner as Barney dropped
into the chair opposite him. "We're not going to
have time for a long chatty lunch after all.

Although you're welcome to tool over to Southport with me after a quick meal."

"Why Southport."

Clearing his throat, Banner said, "Since winning my latest Katzie, my stock has gone up
again. One of the many accolades is going to be
a special show of my originals at Jocko Pease's
Graphic Arts Museum."

"That's practically like being hung in the
Louvre."

"I'll sidestep the obvious rejoinder." Banner
picked up his martini. "Jocko's problem is that
most of his near-priceless Banner originals went
up in smoke during the recent conflagration. I
am going to loan him a batch from my own
trove." He sipped at the drink. "Hell, I've got
more than three thousand of the damn things."

"Aren't fans continually begging you for
them?"

"Beggars I don't mess with. You want an
autographed Ty Banner 'Dr. Judge's Family'
original and it's fifty bucks up front. The Sundays are a real bargain at seventy-five."

"How many do you sell?"

"So far this year five."

The waiter appeared and Barney ordered a
Perrier. "The reason I wanted to talk to you,
Ty, is—"

"You're better off ordering plain club soda,
old pal. All these fancy bubbling waters are—"

"I know, people keep telling me that." He

leaned his elbows on the checkered tablecloth. "You're fairly close to the Judd family."

Banner said, "I haven't seen Archie for aeons. Russ and I play a little golf now and then, I've had lunch with him and the lovely Beth at the rate of about once every six months. I keep in touch with them by phone, but I'm not what you call an intimate. Why?"

Do you think something could've happened to Archie? Something they're hiding? No, he couldn't come out and ask it that way. "I'm sort of concerned about Archie," he began finally. "I've been ghosting the strip for a spell and the old man doesn't seem to be improving any."

"He's nearly in his eighties," reminded Banner, studying the river. "When you get that ancient, you can't fight off things very well. Which is why, old buddy, I plan to die at an early age of all the vices I can crowd into my schedule."

Barney tapped the side of the glass the waiter had just brought. His fingers traced zigzags down the condensation. "What would happen if Archie died?"

"It would give the Newspaper Artists Guild an excuse to stage one hell of a wake."

"I mean about the strip, about 'Poor Little Pearl.' "

"Like most of us serfs, despite his clout, Archie has a standard contract with I.F.S.," said Banner. "When he dies, before he's even cold, all rights to the feature revert to Independent. A few fortunate chaps, me not among them, have been able to cajole a survivors clause out of their respective syndicates. When they go on to glory their wives and kin will keep getting a little something off their features. A pittance in most cases, though possibly enough to keep the kids out of the poorhouse.''

"Archie doesn't have a clause like that?"

"Nope." Banner shook his handsome head. "I know for a fact he doesn't. Archie is of the old school. He's always, despite his skinflint qualities and noted feistiness, felt about I.F.S. the way the natives feel about Tarzan. He might even call old Langendorf 'bwana' when they meet. Anyway, he's been content to settle for a fifty-fifty split. In his case that's meant one hell of a lot of money."

"This new musical could bring in even more."

"Sure, a friend of mine is basking in Majorca on his ten percent of a Broadway hit," said Banner. "The Judds could clear possibly a thou a week on the TV series, too. On top of which, there'll be even more loot coming in from the new merchandising the musical and the series will inspire. For years I've been trying to interest anybody in just one little Dr. Judge doll or toy, but when you're locked into stark realism and sophisticated—"

"If Archie dies then, none of the money comes in."

"Not to Beth and Russ, no. It zips instead, all of it, every penny, into the syndicate coffers." Leaning back, Banner scanned his friend's face. "Why all this interest in financial affairs of the Judds?"

Barney said, "Well, being around Beth I—"

"Ah, my scheme is bearing fruit." Banner grinned. "You are falling for the lass."

"I like her, sure, but I was—"

"Have no fear, Archie's been raking it in and salting it away for half a century," Banner told him. "Even if, perish the thought, he expired tomorrow, he's already earned millions. Beth can well afford to keep you."

"I'm not interested in living off her money," Barney said. "By the way, when was the last time you actually saw—"

"Don't let me rush you, Barney, but if we're going to drive over to Jocko's museum and get my masterworks set up before the crowds burst in, you'll have to order now."

"YEAH, IT IS DAMN LUCKY I wasn't in it." Jocko Pease ran a hand through his shaggy hair, then pointed at the ruined automobile.

The car was a great lump of twisted, blackened and now rusting metal. It lay amid a tumble of charred beams and blackened metal rods. Stretching away behind it was a quarter of a block of similar ruin. The skeleton of the cartoon-museum warehouse had been toppled

over after the fire. Burned timbers, buckled
hunks of metal siding, smoked shards of window glass lay in a sooty confusion atop soggy
lumps of black that had once been drawings.

"This still smells like the biggest barbecue in
the world," observed Banner, holding the pile
of his drawings closer to his chest.

"Your car exploded, too?" asked Barney.

Jocko nodded. "Stupid is what I was," he
said, shaking his big head. "That damned Datsun is what started this whole bloody mess. See,
it was a sort of chilly night that particular night.
Least I was feeling chilly, so I had the heaters
on a little. I was only going to pop into the museum for a minute to gather up some publicity
flyers I'd forgotten. I left the damn car idling in
the garage there and went on into the museum.
I wasn't inside for more than a minute or two
when I heard this tremendous *wham*! I come
running out, there's the garage all in flames,
fire roaring up twenty feet."

"Since the garage is attached to the warehouse," said Banner, "that caught fire, too."

"You should've seen me," Jocko went on. "I
ran into the museum again, grabbed up a couple
of dinky fire extinguishers and phoned the fire
department. Hell, squirting that fire didn't do a
damn thing. Then I hoped maybe I could run
around to the other entrance to the warehouse,
you know, and save at least some of the drawings. Maybe the Heinrich Kleys or a 'Little

Nemo' page. When I got to the door, it wasn't a door it was a wall of flame. I expected some guy with a pitchfork to invite me in.''

Turning away from the ruins to look at the museum itself, Banner said, ''At least you saved the museum, Jocko.''

''Yeah, but I hated to see all those beautiful drawings go. Did you see what they are now? Big wads of ashes.''

Barney asked, ''Why did the car catch fire?''

''Fire marshall thinks it must've been a spark or something,'' answered Jocko. ''Must've ignited the gas fumes somehow. I don't know. The insurance people think that's what happened, too. There wasn't any sign of tampering or anything, and the Mafia usually fires restaurants and not art museums anyway. I don't know, it was just an accident. A damn lousy accident.'' He gestured at the black ruins. ''Sure, they'll eventually pay what the drawings were worth, but how the hell can I replace what was lost?''

''Everything turns to ashes sooner or later,'' said Banner. ''How many of my things were lost?''

''I had seven Sunday pages, beautiful stuff,'' said Pease. ''Another thing is, I can't get this wreckage hauled away. The car-insurance bastards won't take the car till the building-insurance people take the debris. And vice versa. So what I have to stare at every day is a reminder of what a jerk I was.''

"C'mon, Jocko," said Banner. "Everybody has left a car idling for a few minutes. You didn't expect it to explode, for Christ's sake."

"If only I'd turned off the ignition."

"Then maybe it would've blown up later, with you in it."

"Sure sure. But it really hurts, losing all that great artwork." Pease started up the curving brick path to the museum proper.

The building was a three-story Victorian-style house, sitting on a knoll and surrounded by three acres of grass and trees. It had recently been painted white, its shutters a pale gold.

"Think how much worse you'd feel if the warehouse were still there and you were incinerated." Banner put a hand on the man's broad back and followed him inside.

Barney took another look at the ruins before he went in after them. There was a large circular foyer floored in real marble. Through one of the open doorways he spotted a large, framed original by Robert Fawcett, one of the illustrators he'd admired when he was learning to draw. "Is that a display of magazine illustration in there?" he asked the shaggy curator.

"Huh? Oh, sure, we're running a display of the golden age of American magazine illustration all this month," Pease replied. "Would've been even better, but some of my 1920s examples burned."

"Mind if I look at it?"

"Go ahead, the museum doesn't open for another hour, so you'll have the show all to yourself."

Banner said, "Trot along, old buddy. Jocko and I will set up this display of the golden age of Ty Banner. That age, I do believe, ended sometime last week. We're into the silver age now. Or maybe brass."

Hands in pockets, Barney entered the big circular room. When the museum had been a home, this was probably the music room. Now the walls were covered with framed drawings and paintings.

Barney was somewhat surprised to discover he could still be excited at seeing the work of such illustrators as these. There was a fantastic Noel Sickles color illustration from the old *Saturday Evening Post*, a terrific Fawcett Civil War drawing, an impressive Austin Briggs sketch of two men walking along Madison Avenue. A simple drawing, but everything about it was right. Even the attitudes of the background figures were perfect.

"Damn it," he said, "what the hell am I doing?"

Drawing lobstermen, human beasts, wide-eyed waifs and idiotic Indian mystics who can't even put their turbans on straight. It's no good, and it's no fun.

When he'd done the kind of illustration he wanted to, even though the money sometimes hadn't been as good, there was a feeling of . . . .

"Look at the dates on this stuff," he reminded himself. "Forties, fifties, few from the sixties. It's all over. There's not that much illustration work anymore, not for the kind of thing you love."

Golden ages were always sometime else, you always missed getting in on them.

Shrugging, he turned his back on the room and left the exhibit.

9

"I DON'T KNOW much about your private life," said Beth.

I don't know much about yours, I don't even know what you've done with Archie. "What aspect of it?"

The girl was sitting in one of the wicker chairs in the big studio. She looked incredibly pretty tonight. "What you do with your weekends. I don't like to impose on you, but. . . ."

If she were funny looking, would he still be here? Probably so, since he still needed the extra six hundred a week. Yeah, even if he weren't falling in love with this girl he'd keep coming around. Besides, he wasn't sure, not completely, that anything had happened to the old cartoonist. Could be there was a simple explanation about. . . .

"This coming weekend?" she was asking him.

His chair squeaked when he straightened up. "I didn't quite catch your entire question, Beth."

"Something causing you to fret?"

"No, no," he lied. "Guess I was still thinking about the new 'Pearl' plot line your dad told me at dinner. Kicking it around."

"You don't like the story?"

"Does sound a little different from the usual 'Poor Little Pearl' continuities. You sure your readers will buy Uncle Goodworx going into the space-colony business?"

Beth said, "A lot of people are interested in alternate life-styles these days. Father thinks Uncle Goodworx, being one of the wealthiest industrialists in America, ought to be in the forefront of new thinking. We did a solar-energy story last year and it pulled nothing but favorable mail. We even picked up three new papers in California."

"What was it you were asking about this weekend?"

"You can draw a space colony, can't you? That's not why you—"

"I can draw anything I'm called on to draw," he said evenly.

"Sorry, I didn't mean to needle you. It's just that dad's very up about this idea, and so am I."

"Archie, too?"

"Yes, he is," she answered. "Grandfather's made quite a reputation for being controversial. Uncle Goodworx built the first atomic-energy plant in this country."

"About the weekend?"

"There's going to be a comic-fans convention of some sort taking place in Boston this weekend," she said. "Where people come to buy comic books, originals and such. They also have guests from the cartoon and comic-book field. They want to present Archie with some kind of cup for his fifty years of continuous service to comic art."

Barney watched her face. "He's going to make the trip?"

"No, he just isn't up to the strain," she said. "Since we'd tentatively agreed when they invited us months ago, we think someone from the family ought to be there. I'm the one who's going. Would you like to come along?"

"Yes, I would. What sort of ceremonies do they have in mind?"

"A luncheon I think, where the various guests get awards. The convention's at the Hotel Cosgrove, in Copley Plaza. Near the Sheraton and all those glass buildings."

"Do I come as a friend of the family or as Archie's assistant?"

"We're not hiding the fact you work on 'Pearl,'" she said. "Besides I'm sure they'll want someone who can draw a few pictures of Pearl for the fans."

"How do we travel?"

"I'll be driving my Porsche," she said. "You may as well come with me, unless you think you'll need your own car."

"My car won't survive a three- or four-hour drive, so I'll come along with you."

"I was at a comics convention in Manhattan

couple years back, so I know what to expect."
She paused, a slight frown on her face. "You
sure you don't mind doing this? I don't want to
foul up your social life, or your deadlines with
Maximus."

"My social life can't be fouled up, and I'm
ahead on everything." Mainly because he
hadn't been sleeping much. An hour after turning in, most nights, Barney would sit up wide
awake and start thinking about Beth and her
grandfather. He would shift all the impressions
he'd gathered, the few real facts, struggling to
come up with an answer. An answer that would
allow him to keep working for Beth and her
father, keep feeling fond of the girl. He used
the sleepless hours, when the thinking was
over, to draw.

"There's an air of sadness about you tonight," Beth told him.

"Actually I'm happy as a clam—make that a
lobster," he said. "Although when I was out
visiting Jocko Pease's museum yesterday I got
to feeling rather forlorn."

"About all the valuable drawings that were
lost?"

"Mostly about how my stuff'll never get included in any exhibit of the great illustrators of
the day."

"You will be, eventually."

"That wasn't the feeling I got yesterday."

She came over to sit beside him on the rattan

sofa. It made another crackling screech. "As much as we need you, Barney, you can quit anytime you want to. Don't think you owe us something, or that I want to keep you from doing the sort of work you really—"

"It isn't you that's keeping me from it. I'm the one," he said. "When I first married Tawny I really felt I'd made a tremendous step ahead. Except about then I...started to...I couldn't seem to keep pushing the way I had...I started taking the easier jobs, the ones that paid more."

"There's nothing wrong with sitting on the sidelines once in a while."

She was close to him, he seemed to be able to feel the glow of her. He put his hands on her shoulders, very gently pulled her to him and kissed her.

Beth murmured; her arms moved around him, tightening.

Barney touched her cheek with his fingertips. "Beth, I—"

Something rustled outside the studio, a branch snapped.

He stood. "Somebody's prowling outside," he said.

She glanced at the row of dark windows. "Probably only an animal—raccoon or something."

"Back in a minute." He ran to the door at the rear of the room.

Through that and he was in a corridor that led

to the doorway outside. He jogged along, pushed out into the darkness.

Yeah, there was the lurker again. Barney could see him now as he untangled himself from the hedges alongside the studio. The figure began a dash for the woods.

"Hold on, you bastard!" Barney sprinted after him.

He caught up, threw himself and tackled the man around the knees.

They both went slamming down on the crunchy gravel, rolled, kneeing and elbowing each other, swearing.

When he was on top again, Barney yanked free. He grabbed the lurker by the front of his dark ski sweater and pulled him upright.

"Watch who you're grabbing, schmuck," warned the big blond man.

It was Jape Easter, the guy Barney'd almost tangled with at the Newspaper Artists Guild banquet, the night he'd met Beth.

Easter, puffing, threw a punch.

Barney let go of him, shoved and dodged. He dealt a chopping flat-hand blow to the man's thick neck.

Easter bellowed, "Oof!" Very much like the lobstermen when the Human Beast got in a good one.

While the big man was still staggering, Barney used his arm as a lever and threw Easter against the nearest maple tree.

That caused Easter to squat suddenly on the ground.

"Suppose," said Barney, stalking toward him, breathing hard, "you tell me why the hell you've been hanging around here."

"Suppose you take a flying leap at a doughnut."

"I'm asking you something!" Barney lunged, caught the sweater again.

"Okay, okay, let's not go fifteen rounds, huh?" Easter got to his feet, put a hand out to ease Barney back. "In the first place, I haven't been hanging around."

"Bullshit, this is the third time I've seen you."

"Not me, babe." Easter shook his head, scowling. "I do admit I was doing some eavesdropping tonight. But never before. You and Beth are pretty close now, huh? Time was—"

"Why are you here at all?"

"I'm an old friend of Beth's." He brushed at his denim trousers. "Before you cut me off, she and I were close. Damn close."

"That's why you were peeping in the window?"

"I drove over tonight to see if I could persuade her to drop you off the strip and let me take over the ghosting for a while," Easter told him. "I got a look at your first week of proofs and they stink. I could do—"

"That doesn't explain why you were prowling."

" I didn't know you were here till I parked. I decided to scout around after I saw that beat-up VW of yours, see how things were before I announced my arrival. That's all."

"Okay, maybe that explains tonight," said Barney. "It sure doesn't explain why you were hanging around here the other times."

"There weren't any other times," insisted Easter, making a low growling sound in his chest. "Take out your paranoia on somebody else."

"Maybe the police can get a little more out of you."

"What are you going to tell the cops? That I'm not allowed to call on my old girl friend?"

"Housebreaking's a nice charge. The other day you—"

"Listen, asshole, I haven't been here in months," said Easter. "And I sure as hell don't need your permission to see Beth tonight."

"Good evening, Jape." Beth, a cardigan over her slim shoulders, was coming toward them. "Was there something you wanted?"

Easter sucked in a slow, angry breath. "No, I guess not," he said. "But if you want some quality back in your life, you know where to find me." He went stomping away into the night.

"Good night," the girl said.

Barney put an arm around her. "Listen, Beth, I think you ought to report him to the police. The idea of somebody like Easter hanging around here at night . . . ."

"He won't do it again," she said.

They heard Easter's car door slam, the motor roar to life. The car went screeching away along the driveway out front.

"Is that guy really an old boyfriend of yours?"

"Afraid so," she admitted as they walked back to the studio. "You can like all sorts of odd things when you're young."

THE BIG KITCHEN smelled pleasantly of nutmeg. Beth, resting her hip against the circular marble-top table, sipped at her cup of eggnog. "There's something else I ought to tell you," she said.

Barney's grip on his mug tightened. Was this going to be a confession about what was really going on? "Having to do with Jape Easter?" he managed to make himself ask.

"No, there's really nothing much more to talk about in that area," she said. "That disaster area. Looking back, I realize Jape was a good deal more interested in ingratiating himself with my grandfather than he was in romancing me. I was really quite dopey, good thing you didn't meet me back then."

"He acts as though he was jealous of me. Indicating passion of some sort."

"I imagine he's hot to ghost the strip. It's your

involvement with Pearl, not with me, that annoys him."

"Still think a word to the cops would help."

Shaking her head, Beth said, "Not necessary, really. Now, listen, there's something I think I'd better tell you."

Here it comes. Do I really want to hear this? "You don't owe me any—"

"An opportunity's coming up," the girl told him. "Something I don't want to pass up. A potential opportunity actually. Knowing how you feel about this sort of thing, I wanted to warn you in advance. In case something does come of it. Anyway, I'm going into Manhattan tomorrow...to try out for a part...in a TV commercial." She hurried the final words out. "There."

He blinked. "That's what you wanted to tell me?"

"You've given me every indication you think acting on televison, even in a commercial spot, is one or two steps below hustling on street corners. So I felt I ought to tell you what I plan to do."

"Actually I don't feel as violently as I did," he admitted. "Although I would hate to see you go the way of Tawny."

"No fear," she said, laughing. "I'm not exactly built along the lines of your wife."

"Ex-wife," he corrected. "What's the account?"

"Marcus Coffee," she answered. "I'm auditioning for the part of a young suburban housewife whose brilliant architect husband is growing cold and distant because she can't serve him a decent cup of java in the morning. Typical suburban domestic problem, as you well know."

"Yep, bad coffee has ruined many a household."

She looked directly into his face. "You won't be greatly unsettled if I were to get the part?"

"Will you be?"

"No, I'd really love it."

"Then fine."

She held the warmth of the cup against her cheek for a few seconds before turning it to set it on the table. "That idiotic Jape really messed up an otherwise pleasant evening."

"We could try to revive it." Placing his cup next to hers, he put an arm around her.

"I probably taste like eggnog."

"No matter." He kissed her.

10

THE DOCTOR WHEEZED. "Does it hurt down here?"

"No, only higher up," answered Barney.

Dr. Emerson straightened up and tottered away from the examining table. He was a fat man in his late sixties, his head decorated with standing wisps of fine white hair. "You can get dressed now, Mr. King."

"Kains." Barney pulled up his trousers, tucked in his shirt.

"Kains, of course." The old doctor sank into a metal chair. Behind him a small window showed one branch of a blossoming tree. "You seem to be suffering from what I like to call cartoonist's back."

"Is it serious?"

"Not especially. Comes from sitting on your fanny too much."

"What would you suggest?"

The old doctor was feeling at the pockets of his rumpled white jacket. "Right now I'll prescribe something for the pain." He located his prescription pad and commenced searching for a pen. "Over the long haul, Mr. King, I strongly advise exercise. Your fanny's too wide already, best do something about it while you can."

Automatically feeling his backside, Barney said, "It is?" There really wasn't supposed to be anything wrong with him; the back pains he'd invented to give him an excuse for talking to the Judd family doctor.

Wheezing, Dr. Emerson scribbled two lines on the prescription memo. "Sitting too much, boozing too much," he said, "that's what kills most of them in your line of work. Plus a suicide now and then."

"You treat quite a few artists and cartoonists."

"In my time I have." The old doctor sighed to his feet and tore off the prescription. "I've outlived a flock of them. Famous artists, famous cartoonists, famous writers. If they'd paid more attention to my advice, they might be alive yet."

"How about Archie Judd?"

Dr. Emerson looked over his shoulder at the morning outside. "Archie's one of the smart ones," he answered. "He gets plenty of fresh air and exercise on that bicycle of his. He only drinks in moderation. The man could live to be ninety."

I wouldn't bet on it. "As I told you, I work for

Archie." Barney hopped off the table, causing the white paper to crinkle. "He seems to be taking a long time to get over this flu of his."

"That's to be expected." Dr. Emerson wobbled over to hand him the prescription. "Don't take too much of this stuff, it might make you goofy. Lots of these crazy Westport high-school kids eat this stuff as if it was candy."

Barney accepted the slip. "You must be one of the few doctors hereabouts who still makes house calls."

"You have to with a case like Archie's. Can't have him coming out, straining himself."

"You see him pretty often?"

"Every other day." Dr. Emerson took hold of the doorknob.

"So you saw him yesterday?"

"Day before. I'm due to drop in again right after lunch." He pulled open the examining room door. "You're very concerned about him."

"When you work for a man, you're naturally interested in his well-being."

"No need to worry, Archie'll pull out of this," said the old doctor. "Give him my best wishes when you see him."

"I will, sure."

Barney made his way to the small parking lot behind this section of brown shingle building. A beer truck was grunting up the incline of Route

33, a splendidly tanned man in a fresh new scarlet warm-up suit was jogging enthusiastically downhill, birds were twittering in the branches above his old dusty Volkswagen.

"He's lying, too," said Barney as he drove away.

HE SETTLED his possibly ailing backside onto the train seat, after arranging his portfolio next to him. Barney's foot tapped a discarded beer can on the floor, causing it to go bowling down the aisle. If this 10:35 did a really good job he'd be in Manhattan by 11:40 or so. That'd give him time to deliver this latest batch of Human Beast pages to Carlotsky, listen to a few minutes of his editor's ranting and raving and still keep his 12:30 lunch date with Texaco.

The car doors wheezed shut, the Conrail train eased out of the Westport Station.

Something made Barney turn and look out his streaked window toward the slowly vanishing platform.

Jape Easter was standing out there, leaning against a billboard for *Forbes* magazine and making no effort to catch this train. He was staring right at Barney, an odd smile on his thick face.

"Jerk," mouthed Barney before turning away.

Why was the guy following him?

Maybe he wasn't.

Jape lived somewhere in the vicinity of the train station, so it could be he was just out for exercise. You know, getting the fresh air and exercise that old quack Emerson recommends.

That was a strange smile, though. Smug. Leering.

Has Beth told you everything about that bastard, about what went on between them?

Okay, so possibly she slept with the guy once. Or twice.

We're living in the waning years of the twentieth century after all.

Yeah, but Jape Easter. How could she go to....

Suppose she had to? Yeah, suppose that schmuck has been blackmailing her? Could be, hell, he still is. That's why he lurks around the mansion, that's why he tails you.

He may know where Archie is.

The train shuddered and squeaked to a stop on the South Norwalk Station. Barney glanced out at the mixture of tumbled slum houses and new shopping malls.

He attempted to distract himself by reading what had been scrawled on the tan, plastic seat cover in front of him. Rothenstein Sucks!

The Stones are Still Great!

Debbi Will Do It. Not bad lettering on that last one.

Barney reached into his portfolio, remembering he'd promised Carlotsky some rough sketches for the next "Human Beast" cover. He opened his sketchbook, rested it on his lap and took a black Stylist pen out of his sport-coat pocket.

Okay, Dr. Emerson gave you a line of crap. Archie isn't up in that bedroom at all, so there's no way the old medico can be visiting him there.

Had Dr. Emerson botched something, an operation or a prescription? Killed the old cartoonist by accident?

But why would the Judds help cover that up?

You really couldn't trust a doctor who was sick himself. Physician heal thyself and all. And Emerson's wheeze sounded like he was in bad shape.

Okay, but where is Archie?

Beth must know. Did she and Jape Easter. . . .

Barney shook his head, striving to get rid of all the conflicting suspicions that were rattling around up there.

He noticed he'd drawn the Human Beast with Jape's blond head.

He turned to a fresh page.

Let's see, some kind of aliens are attacking San Francisco. Wasn't that what Carlotsky had suggested? Right, they were sharkmen from another dimension and they, for some reason Barney couldn't at the moment recall, had decided to eat the Golden Gate Bridge. An iron deficiency maybe. The Human Beast has to stop them.

The way Jape Easter had been smiling. . . . I bet that bastard did sleep with her.

Concentrate on the task at hand.

"Are you an artist?"

He looked up and across the aisle. "Beg pardon?"

A plump woman in a plain cloth coat was smiling tentatively at him. "I'm an art student myself, in an adult-ed course, and I thought perhaps you might be a fellow artist." She gestured at the sketchbook in his lap.

"No, just a doodler. Actually I'm a certified public accountant." He shut the book, hung the pen back in his pocket and dropped the sketchbook away into his portfolio.

Noticing a discarded magazine under his left foot, he bent and scooped it up.

It was *People* and smiling at him from the cover was Tawny. She looked quite stunning in a three-piece swimsuit.

Barney dropped the magazine back to the floor, shut his eyes and pretended to be asleep for the rest of the ride into Grand Central.

"NOT THAT ONE, the blonde. How could a brunette look like a young Louise Allbritton?" Texaco lifted the top half of his hamburger bun, ladled out relish from the pseudopewter bowl.

"The slim, cool blonde in the second booth from the door."

Barney didn't turn to look. "I guess she does."

"One doesn't come upon Louise Allbritton look-alikes every day here in the Apple," Texaco continued. "Evelyn Ankers quite a lot, but not Louise Allbritton. And how come you ain't your usual euphoric self today, amigo?"

"I went to see a doctor this morning."

His curly-haired friend looked concerned. "You sick or something? Have you caught what Archie Judd has, or are you on the brink of a collapse like Warloff?"

"Neither, I'm perfectly fine. Well, my ass is too wide, but I can live with that."

"A sturdy butt is what guys in our line need. Why, then, are you downcast?"

Barney hesitated, looking around the crowded hamburger restaurant. He took a sip of his club soda. He tapped the lip of his pseudo-pewter plate. "It's nothing," he said.

"I assumed, after your audience with Carlotsky today, you would be elated at least. He's decided to keep you on the Human Beast, he's going to give you a spot in the *Grim Tales* black-and-white magazine, and best of all, he's going to stick poor Tandofsky with Peter Pupp instead of you."

"I am elated."

"Hey, look at that lady going by out there on

Lex. An exact duplicate of Olivia de Havilland.''

"Maybe it is Olivia de Havilland.''

"Naw, she's a plump old broad now. I'm talking about the Olivia de Havilland who exists only on aging celluloid. The one Errol Flynn was always trying to get at.'' He sent a hand across the table. "Are you going to eat those corn chips?''

"Nope, you can have them.''

"How about the pickle?''

"That, too.''

"Much obliged.'' The cartoonist gathered the borrowed food onto his plate and began eating it. "So you're heading for Boston tomorrow?''

"Yep.''

"I can tell by your face you're overjoyed at the prospect of journeying to Beantown.''

"I am, yeah.''

"A weekend with Beth Judd would sure cheer me up, and clear out my nasal passages,'' said Texaco. "She looks an awful lot like the young Audrey Hepburn.''

"No, she doesn't.''

"For an artist, you have a rotten eye.''

Barney tried a little of the club soda. "Listen, Texaco, we've been friends for quite a few years.''

"Since the days when you were a virtuous commercial artist and hadn't fallen into the clutches of Carlotsky.''

"You're about the only guy I can trust, or one of the few," he went on. "Out in Westport I can probably trust Ty Banner, except he's too close to this thing."

"Want me to slip into my robes before you make your confession?"

"There's something...."

"It has to do with Beth?"

"With her and... the whole family."

Texaco stopped eating, lowering an untasted chip to his plate. "You're really taken with her, aren't you? I haven't seen that glassy stare in your orbs since back when you were possessed with Tawny mania," he said. "Okay, you have fallen in love with Beth but there's some obstacle. Is that it?"

"You could put it that way. I really can't go into the details, not many of them. I'm pretty sure, damn sure, Beth's been lying to me."

"About another guy?" inquired Texaco. "Surely you're not still moping about competition from Jape Easter?"

"Not really, no," answered Barney. "Although I'm still pretty curious about what he's up to. This morning he was on the platform at Westport."

Texaco thrust a forefinger into the air. "Perhaps, Holmes, the bloke wanted to catch a train."

"That's just it, Texaco, he didn't. Just stood on the platform looking at me funny."

"Did you happen to ask this doctor you consulted if you might be suffering from galloping paranoia, amigo? Listen, Jape Easter looks at everybody funny, it has to do with the structure of what passes for his head."

"He had a smug expression on his damn face."

"When you've got a brain the size of his, you're very easily pleased. Doesn't take much to make a lout like J.P. appear pleased." Texaco picked up the chip. "Is all your brooding centered on this clunk's facial expressions?"

"The main thing worrying me is the fact I'm pretty certain Beth's been lying to me."

"You're absolutely sure?"

"Not completely, no."

"But this has nothing to do with her romantic life?"

"Nope."

Texaco sat silent for a few seconds. "You're not using our comradeship to the fullest," he said finally. "I get the feeling you're a long way from confiding in me. Makes it very tough for me to make like Ann Landers or Siggy Freud."

"I know, but I can't get any more specific. Not yet."

Texaco ate the chip. "Okay, then you have got two basic courses to follow," he advised. "You either ask Beth point-blank to clear up what's bothering you or you poke around on

your own until you find out the answers.
Whichever way, you'll get at the truth."

"Right, I'll have to do that."

"Which?"

"Maybe both," replied Barney.

.

THE WESTPORT LIBRARY was a few minutes
from closing. Barney was up in the second-floor
stacks, rummaging through the books on California for some acceptable shots of the Golden
Gate Bridge. There wasn't much in the scrap
file in his studio and Carlotsky was insisting on
the bridge's being an essential ingredient of the
next "Human Beast" cover.

"Maybe I ought to fly out to Frisco for a first-
hand look," he said to himself as he turned
pages. "Get away from here altogether for a
spell, before I find out anything else."

He couldn't do that. There was no way he
could desert Beth.

Here was an appetizing four-color photo of
the Golden Gate Bridge. He tilted the open book
so the overhead light hit it full.

Someone touched him in the small of the
back.

Barney spun.

"Wow, you have very good reflexes." Beth
was standing at the entrance to the row of
stacks, very pretty in jeans, plaid shirt and cardigan.

"And you're very quiet on your feet."

"I saw you up here from down in the music room," the girl explained. "I did some silent waving, even tried E.S.P. You noticed me not at all."

"I'm a few months behind on my E.S.P. bill, think they maybe turned it off. How are you?"

"I'm elated," she answered, smiling at him.

Barney asked, using that murmuring voice you affect in public places that require quiet, "Has to do with that coffee commercial you auditioned for?"

Beth took hold of his hand, squeezing. "I got it, Barney. I got the part," she said. "They phoned me just an hour ago. I felt so up I had to get out of the house for a while. Tried to phone you, but you weren't home."

"That's great news," he said. "But since you're the perfect suburban-housewife type, it comes as no surprise."

"They're shooting it early next month," she told him. "You ought to see the fellow who's going to be my husband. Six foot three, tan as a lifeguard, has blond hair that must give high-school girls palpitations."

"You're immune?"

"So far, and besides he's almost certainly gay," she said. "You really are pleased?"

"I am, yeah, long as you are," he said. "I decided you aren't likely to let this sort of thing make you goofy in the way my . . . ."

how come I recognize you. You know, Mr. Kains, you are really great.''

"Well, thanks.''

"You want a discount on any Golden Age magazines, see me.''

"Which golden age is this?''

"Nineteen thirty-eight, you know, until 1942. Some dealers call it the golden age way up to 1948. But that ain't no golden age, that was all over by '42.''

The elevator thunked to a stop, the doors hissed open on the mezzanine.

"Nice meeting you,'' Barney said as the black man pushed out into the milling crowd.

There were at least a hundred people moving through the area around the bank of elevators, pushing toward the entrances to various rooms. An immense floor-to-ceiling window, tinted pale blue, showed the insurance-company towers outside and a strip of the Charles River.

Beth took his hand. "Weren't you expecting to be recognized by your fans?''

"I wasn't even aware I had any. Where are we supposed to report?''

"I have to find a man named Martin Phelps. He's the one in charge of putting on this whole mess.''

Three pudgy teenage boys in T-shirts brushed by. One of them whispered something and they slowed. They halted, the pudgiest one came back to Barney.

"Are you Barney Kains?"

"Yes. Are you Martin—"

"Will you sign this?" Stuffing a plastic bag loaded with comic books under his arm, he thrust a thin convention program and a ballpoint pen at Barney. "They didn't even announce you were going to be here. Typical of the half-ass way Phelps runs—"

"Could you autograph mine, too, Mr. Kains?" Another of the boys was holding out a booklet and a pen.

"I hear you're going to be doing stuff for *Grim Tales*."

"I am, but how'd you fellas find—"

"Could you do a sketch of H.B. for me?"

Barney nodded toward Beth. "Can you wait a minute while I oblige?"

"Sure, go ahead." She smiled. "Maybe they'd like a drawing of 'Poor Little Pearl,' too."

"That crap?" said one of the pudgy boys.

"Garbage," remarked another.

"What do you have to do with 'Poor Little Pearl'?"

"I'm drawing. . . assisting on it."

"Why?"

Barney started a very rough sketch of his hero in his beast phase. "Mostly because I've fallen hopelessly in love and want to save all the money I can so I can buy a vine-covered—"

"No, seriously, Mr. Kains, an artist with your potential shouldn't be wasting his time on junk."

"You're better than Jack Kirby."

"As good as Steranko."

Finishing up the drawing and the autographs, he returned programs and pens. "Thanks, fellas."

"Are you going to be on one of the discussion panels?"

"That's one of the things we're trying to discover."

"We'll come and listen if you are."

"Most of the panels suck. But we'll go to yours."

He returned to Beth, dodging a bearded young man who was carrying a stack of coverless comic books. "Let's continue our search for this guy Phelps."

"You don't think Pearl is junk, do you?"

"Don't pay attention to fans." He noticed a door marked Convention Committee. "Let's try over there."

"Know where I can sell this?" A thin old man in a heavy khaki overcoat held up a battered copy of *Looney Tunes*. "I hear these fools pay thousands of dollars for old funny books."

Twisting, nodding to his left, Barney said, "That seems to be the dealers' room over there, the big one that says Benjamin Franklin Ballroom next to the doors."

"You wouldn't want to buy it, would you? Make me an offer of more than five hundred dollars."

"Sorry, I only collect Golden Age." He guided

Beth through the doorway of the committee room.

There was only a fat young man in a T-shirt in there, seated behind a card table. He was making notes in a big yellow tablet that rested next to a wedge of cold pizza. "Committee only in here," he said without raising his eyes. "If you need tickets you have to go—"

"I'm Barney Kains, this is Bethany Judd. She's an invited guest and we'd like to find out where—"

"You're almost late," the fat boy told Barney, looking up at him now. "Your panel starts in about three minutes."

"What panel?"

"Just a minute." He reached across the pizza to grab a sheaf of mimeographed pages. "This is Saturday, right? I lose all track of time being. . . . Yeah, here you are, Barney. 'The Comic Strip Today.' That's in the Bunker Hill Room."

"Somebody is supposed to give Miss Judd a cup for her grandfather. Where do—"

"That's not until tomorrow." He located a sheet of green mimeo paper, held it up to them. "See, Final Luncheon, 1:00 P.M., Sunday. Boston Tea Party Room."

Beth asked, "Could I talk to Martin Phelps?"

The fat boy chuckled. "It's next to impossible to find him during a con. He's everywhere and nowhere, like a will-o'-the-wisp. You do a damn good job on Human Beast, Barney."

"Thanks, now I—"

"You better get your butt in gear, though. They'll start the panel without you if you don't hurry up. You're supposed to be in the Bunker Hill Room. Take a left before you go into the Huckster Room."

Barney leaned toward the girl. "You want to tag along while I sit in on this panel thing?"

"Of course," she said, smiling. "If I don't have to accept any trophies until tomorrow, I've all sorts of time."

Halfway to the panel room three pudgy boys blocked their path.

"Aren't you Barney Kains?"

"Can you sign our—"

"Didn't I just do that?"

"No, sir."

"Must've been another trio of.... You'll have to catch me later, fellas. They tell me I'm supposed to be doing a panel right now."

"Are you going to discuss your work at Maximus?"

"No, actually I—"

"Right over this way, Barney." Taking hold of him, Beth guided him to a glass-paneled door.

There were two hundred folding chairs set up in the red-carpeted room. Fewer than fifty people, mostly pudgy teenage boys, sat scattered through the room. Up on a makeshift platform three panel members were seated at a long wooden table and sharing one portable microphone.

"Syndicates are always looking for bright new features," an immense woman in a flowered Mother Hubbard was explaining.

"I'll escape soon as I can," Barney whispered.

"Wink when you want me to applaud." She kissed his cheek, and took a chair at the rear of the small auditorium.

Barney, hunched slightly, walked up to the stage. "Excuse me," he said quietly to the chubby, blond young man who might be the moderator. "I'm Barney Kains."

"Great, I'm Willis Folger. Been wanting to meet you, since we both live in Fairfield County. Funny how we had to both come to Boston to—"

"Do you want me to wait until you two have finished your conversation?" asked the fat woman.

"Sorry, Debbie," said Folger. "Hold off a sec. Come on up on the stage, Barney, and take the empty chair. Do you know Bud Heinz?"

"He moved out of Westport before I moved in." He climbed onto the planking, nearly tripped over the mike cord, got himself into the folding metal chair between the fat woman and a lean gray-haired man.

"May I proceed?" the woman asked, taking a displeased puff at her cigarillo.

"Give me the mike a sec," requested Folger,

plump hand grabbing it away from her. He was about twenty-four, decked out in a three-piece blue denim suit.

"I was about to make what I considered an important—"

"One sec, Debbie."

"Ladies and gentlemen," announced Folger, "I'm sure you'll join me in greeting a late but very welcome addition to our little discussion. This gentleman actually had a considerable reputation in the illustration field before he quit to pursue what is, I understand, his first love, namely comic books. You've all seen his brilliant work in the pages of the various Maximus books, most recently as the depictor of the best-selling Human Beast. He is also helping out on one of the major comic strips, which is why we invited him to sit in on this particular panel. He's assistant to my good friend—that giant in the field—Archie Judd. Here's Barney Kains."

The small crowd gave him an unexpected enthusiastic round of applause.

"Now, Barney, let me introduce Debra LaViolet, the very capable comics editor at Impressive Features, Inc., in New York."

The fat woman retrieved the microphone, blew out a tatter of smoke, and spoke. "In answer to the question you asked so long ago, young man, I am always interested in seeing fresh new features at I.F.I. Everything that comes in, whether it's submitted by a so-called old pro or a rank novice, gets my full and. . . ."

Folger rocked back in his chair, reaching around Debra LaViolet to tap Barney. "Beth is here with you, isn't she?"

"Back of the room, yes."

"Great, because I've got a batch of blowups for her," he said. "Pictures I took when Archie and I visited poor Jocko's museum a few weeks back. She'll probably want to see them."

"So will I," said Barney.

12

So this was Archie Judd. A short, thickset man with white hair that stood straight in a sort of exuberant crew cut. His broad nose had been broken once long ago, there was a small scar on his forehead that hiked up his left eyebrow. In the photos he was either standing next to the dedicated young cartoon buff Willis Folger or with the bearish Jocko Pease. In two of the pictures Archie, a disgruntled expression on his wrinkled face, was posing beside a large "Poor Little Pearl" Sunday-page original. The drawing had been placed on an easel in the foyer of the Graphic Arts Museum. The old cartoonist was pointing at the old drawing with one hand while his other twiddled with his wide flying-geese necktie.

This was probably as close to Archie as Barney was ever going to. . . .

He sat up in the armchair. He moved the top photo in the collection Folger had given them over nearer the table lamp. "Something wrong with this," he said half aloud.

"What?" Beth was at the bathroom mirror, the door partly open.

"There's nothing wrong with your grandfather's hands," he said.

"Thought you said something *was* wrong."

"That's what's wrong, nothing is wrong."

Lipstick in hand, the girl looked in at him. "Is that an epigram?"

He studied another picture. "I can't quite remember why," he said, "but.... Nope, can't get it."

Beth appeared in the doorway, head tilted slightly to the right. "Is it something important?"

He stacked the pictures on the hotel room's writing table next to the Gideon Bible. "I'm not even sure of that," he told her. "It occurred to me, for some reason I can't quite get in focus, there ought to be something wrong with one of Archie's hands, some sign of a minor injury. Bandage or gauze."

"He did scrape his hand a few weeks ago, took a small spill off his bicycle."

"When was that?"

"Oh," she answered. "Right before he got sick."

"Before he visited the cartoon museum?"

Beth thought a moment before shrugging. "After all this time I can't remember," she told him finally. "Did you ever think about how much of your life you forget entirely?"

"There are quite a few patches I don't miss."

Clicking off the bathroom light, she came over to sit on the edge of her bed. Behind her the high wide window showed twilight filling in the spaces between the high office buildings and churches; out on the river a solitary rower, almost a ghost in the fading light, was gliding by. "You were absolutely the star of the panel discussion this afternoon," she said.

"I tried to fend 'em off best I could. I wouldn't pay too much attention to what some of the kids said about 'Poor Little Pearl.'"

Beth had left her purse sitting in the middle of the bed. She twisted, reaching back to drop her lipstick in it. Her tan skirt moved up across her slim bare legs. "I think it's valuable to listen to what the public thinks," she said, straightening up. "They sure were flattering to you, if not to Pearl."

"There's a lot, Beth, of mystique that's grown up around the Maximus comics through the years," he tried to explain. "The sort of people you meet at cons—high school and college kids for the most part—don't much care for newspaper strips at all. To them characters such as the Human Beast, Captain Cyclops, Flaming Death and Hyperman are...well, idols, gods almost. Sure, there's almost a religious fervor about it. Naturally when someone like me, practically the Matthew, Mark and whoever of their faith, suggests he may be deserting the shrine

for newspaper work, they're going to be pissed
off. To them your strip is heathen stuff. Their
feelings don't have much to do with whether
it's a good feature or not.''

She rubbed at her knee. "You probably are
wasting your time with us.''

He smiled across at her. The twilight was
seeping into her hotel room, softening everything outside the glow of the single lamp. "Not
with you, Beth," he said. "With Pearl, Goombah, Uncle Goodworx and Muffin maybe, but
not with you.''

"You won't quit?''

Her face looked very sad. "Hey, don't go
turning into Pearl on me." Leaving his chair, he
moved to the bed and put a palm, gently, on
each side of her face.

Beth's hands came up to cover his. "Barney,
sometimes I wish I. . . .''

"Wish what?''

"Nothing," she said, swallowing. "Are you
all that anxious for Japanese food?''

"Not especially." He leaned and kissed her.

"Because I thought," she said after a moment, "we could just as well stay in.''

SKELETONS ON BICYCLES. Pursuing him across a
wintry Boston Common. Barney screamed out
in terror.

But the scream must have sounded only over
there in his nightmare. There wasn't even an

echo of it in the dark bedroom. Beth was still asleep beside him.

He sat there, the thin hotel blanket fallen away from his bare torso, listening to his heart rattling around inside him. He blinked and the slice of moonlight coming in through the nearly closed draperies fragmented into circles of hazy light.

Rubbing his eyes, waggling his jaw, he worked at getting all the aspects of himself under control.

The girl murmured, snuggled her head into her pillow. She was sleeping on her side, one hand fisted under her chin. He watched her naked back, enjoying the smooth loveliness of it.

What a career, what a terrific romantic career. Way back in college it started, when you were smitten with that cheerleader. Can't even remember her name. . .Midge. That's right, Midge Minter. Christ, you should've run like Jim Fixx from a girl who willingly let people call her Midge. A sure symptom of deep trouble upstairs. She certainly had been cute, though, sort of a sexy Doris Day. If that were possible. Unfaithful, though, with enough guys to make up a football team. In fact, some of them were on the football team.

Then there was Tawny—many mistakes later. What a misstep that was. Okay, she's now one of the ten most beautiful women in the world.

Those years with her, though, really fouled you up. Somehow you rode right on by your stop.

You did it to yourself, old buddy. You could have stuck to doing what you loved, no matter what sort of tantrums Tawny staged. Being goofy over her was only your excuse. . .except I wonder now if you ever really loved her at all.

Jesus, why is it at 3:00 A.M. I always end up sounding like continuity out of "Dr. Judge's Family"?

True, though, amigo. I know I love Beth and it's nothing like what I felt about Tawny.

Splendid. True love comes to Bernard Kains as he staggers toward thirty-two. She is special, pretty, bright, loving.

She also, however, has lied to you from the absolute start of all this.

Archie Judd isn't up in that damn bedroom. A bunch of cassette recordings are up there.

Why?

What did they do to the old man? Where is he?

Wait a minute. Remember Texaco's advice.

You have got to ask her.

Here you are in the same bed with the girl. You love her, she loves you.

Let's hope so. Otherwise this would only be a sleazy shackup.

What happened in Boston, Barney?

Quit being so goddamn cynical. She really loves you, you can tell.

How?

Well, for one thing, she told me.

Oh, so? Same way she told you how much Archie liked your work on the strip? Same way she has recounted all the cheery conversations she's had with the old darling up in his sickroom?

Okay, okay, she's lying about that. Doesn't mean she's lying when she tells me how she feels about me.

Fine, we accept the fact she truly loves you. With a deep, unbridled passion.

So what?

What are you going to do? Live with her? Marry her?

How do you get around inviting Archie to the ceremony?

Or maybe when you're on your honeymoon, she'll confess she took an ax to her grandpappy.

No, Beth isn't capable of that kind of violence.

Only of conning you. Only of lying to you, using you because they were in desperate need of someone to come in quick and draw the strip.

If you hadn't obliged, they'd have hired Jape Easter or Jocko Pease or some other hack.

Sure, and right now one of those guys would be sitting here staring at her bare ass.

C'mon, stop it. Beth isn't like that.

She used to sleep with Jape Easter.

I'm not sure of that.

Why is the guy hanging around? Could be he

is still sleeping with Beth. He got his signals
crossed the other night, showed up on a night
when it was your turn.

Concentrate. Rid your brain of all this garbage.

The real problem is this. You have to ask her
where Archie is. Tell her you must know what
happened to him.

Do it now.

Barney let his hand drift toward the girl. It
hovered on her shoulder.

No, he couldn't ask her openly.

His hand dropped.

There was only one other way to find out.

He'd have to dig until he found the answers
on his own.

A THIN SLICE of morning showed through the
draperies. Barney, more or less dressed, was
huddled in an uncomfortable chair in front of
the giant color TV. He had the sound turned low,
so as not to awaken Beth, and was switching
from channel to channel.

"Troops massed for an imminent invasion
that could upset the entire balance of power in
this key area of the world," a lugubrious newscaster with unbelievable hair was saying.

You get used to your own local newscasters
after a while, but out-of-town ones always look
strange and unreal. As alien as lobstermen from
another solar system.

He tried another channel.

Tom was chasing Jerry up a drainpipe.

Better than the voice of doom, but not quite what Barney was in the mood for.

Another channel. An alligator was eating a little boy. More cartoon comedy.

The next channel gave him a cowboy evangelist with a diamond-studded cross decorating his high-crown sombrero. "Ain't no problem Jesus can't tackle," he was twanging. "Lawdie me, I can testify to that. I was loaded down with trouble and tribulations, weighted with the burden of a whole stewpot of problems, an' I just took 'em. . . ."

"Wonder if this guy could solve a murder."

Switching again, Barney found a familiar face on the screen. It was Willis Folger, the cartoon buff, being interviewed on a local Boston talk show.

"Our WEQM viewers must be curious as to why otherwise rational people can lay out good money for this sort of ephemeral garbage," the lean black host was saying.

Folger gave a boyish chuckle. "Is that what they call a loaded question, Gabe?"

"Let me phrase it another way, Willis. If I wanted to invest in comic books and comic art—the kind of junk I saw on display at the comics convention now being held at the Hotel Cosgrove—what would you suggest I put my money into?"

"You're simply talking about an investment, Gabe, and not about something you might actually like?"

"I'm going into it just for the bucks, say."

"Well, I'm not very much into old comic books myself," said Folger, settling into a new position in his tube chair. "I can tell you, however, about comic-art originals... which are a darn good investment. As a hedge against inflation they're terrific, some pieces appreciating incredibly in the past five years or so."

"Now what exactly is an original?"

"Glad you asked, so I can finally show some of these things I brought along."

"I'm the perfect straight man."

Chuckling again, Folger picked a large drawing off the pile resting on the lopsided coffee table beside him. "An original is the page that the cartoonist draws to be engraved," he explained. "You know, the drawing is photographed, engraved and all. Then the syndicate prints up glossy proofs that are the exact size the feature'll be running. Those they mail out to the client newspapers, usually a few days late. When—"

"Too early in the morning for all this technical stuff, Willis. Tell us about that drawing you're clutching in your hot little hand."

"This is one of my all-time favorites, an original 'Prince Valiant' Sunday page by the great Hal Foster."

"It's sure big."

"Hal always did them twice the size they'd be appearing in the Sunday funnies, Gabe."

"What's this particular drawing worth?"

"It's an early page from 1940. Six years ago I paid four hundred dollars for it," he said. "Today at the con someone offered me twelve hundred. I'm not interested in selling, though."

"Quite a jump in price."

"I'd rather look at this than a couple of gold coins or a bar of silver."

"What else have you in that stack?"

"Well, Gabe, this next . . . is the camera getting this?"

"Hold it a tad higher."

"This is a beautiful Milton Caniff Sunday 'Terry And The Pirates' original from 1937. The originals from this period are extremely rare. This one is worth, in today's market, about two thousand dollars."

"He's the guy who does . . . 'Steve Canyon,' isn't he?"

"That's right. You're picking up an education in graphics already, Gabe."

"I learn fast. You say it's rare. How rare?"

"I've only seen a few others. And two of those belonged to a friend of mine, Jocko Pease. They unfortunately were destroyed in a disastrous fire at his cartoon museum in Connecticut a few weeks ago."

"Which makes yours even more valuable, huh?"

"Hadn't thought of that, but you're right. Hate to think of all that nice stuff going up in flames, though."

"What's the top price an original can bring?"

"Oh, I suppose a Winsor McKay 'Little Nemo' or possibly a 'Buster Brown' by Richard Outcault would bring as much as ten thousand dollars," replied Folger. "They both date back to the early years of this century and are tough to come by. Not my favorite period in American cartooning, although I know a bit about it."

"You don't have one of those to show us then?"

Folger shook his head. "Wish I did. Poor Jocko Pease had some fine examples, but they're just ashes now, too."

"I'm glad," said Beth, putting her hand on Barney's shoulder.

He turned the set off, rose to face her. "Glad that the cartoon museum burned down?"

"Nope, glad you're still here." The girl was wearing a short terry-cloth robe, her dark hair tousled. "Pleased you didn't tiptoe out of here while I was sleeping."

He eased his arms around her. "I'm not going away."

"Not yet, anyway."

13

THE AFTERNOON ceased being pleasant a moment after he parked—"concealed" is a better
word—his Volkswagen on the little-used road
behind the Judd estate. Barney had pulled off
the paved road, leaving the car on a patch of
grass surrounded by birch trees. The brush and
trees were thick all around. Across the road the
land slanted down, steep and rocky.

As he began his downhill sneak a chill wind
rose, knifing through the lines of trees, rattling
new leaves, taking away much of the heat of
the afternoon. When he talked to Beth on the
phone a half hour ago, she'd mentioned she and
her father were going to have to spend another
exasperating afternoon at their bank in the
heart of Westport. She also told him Terri
Wormser, the teenager from down the road,
was going to come over to look after Archie.

Doubtful. Since there was no Archie Judd in
the house, there wouldn't be any Terri Wormser, either.

He reached a position in the woods where he

could see the garages. Judging by the limited view the dusty rear windows gave him, Beth's Porsche was at home but not the family Mercedes.

Barney started moving again, walking in an awkward ticktock way down the sharply inclining hillside. At the edge of the woods he halted again. No sign of activity around the mansion. A misplaced seagull was roosting on one of the lopsided weathervanes.

Barney edged along the alleyway between the house and the garage. He was certain no one was inside. Even so, he rang the front doorbell.

He pushed the ivory button a second time, shifting from foot to foot.

The fresh wind was even taking the color out of the day, graying it down.

No answer.

Nodding, Barney jogged around to the rear of the house. There was some precedent for housebreakers using this way in.

He'd done some illustrations once for an article on burglary. This lock looked to be the kind you could get open with a credit card. Those in the break-in trade called the process "loiding," or at least they did back when he'd done the illustrations. Barney had practiced the trick at the time, so he could get the hand gestures and the body attitudes right for one of the drawings. Easing out his wallet, he extracted his Visa card.

Took him thirteen tries before he slid the card just right between jamb and door. Feeling the catch give, he turned the knob and eased the door open. He crossed into the Judd house.

He stood attentively in the big laundryroom, sliding his expired credit card back into the wallet. Everything smelled of pine trees and ammonia back here this afternoon.

He realized he was taking a series of deep, open-mouthed breaths. Closing his mouth, he crossed the room and passed into the corridor beyond.

When he reached the front hall he stopped to look around. No sign or sound of life came to him.

Okay, let's find out about Archie Judd.

Barney bounded up the staircase.

The door to Archie's bedroom was shut today. Not hesitating, Barney opened it and went in.

The bed was still neatly made, the one stereo speaker still sat next to the doorway.

He went, slowly and carefully, around the room. The adjoining bathroom had a cold, mildewed feel. The bristles on the toothbrush in the green plastic glass on the shelf over the basin were dry, caked with yellowed toothpaste.

The shower curtain was pulled closed. After eyeing it, taking in the sea-horse pattern, Barney clutched the thing open. The tub was empty, a tiny circle of rust ringing the drain.

Back in the bedroom he began searching the closets, there were two of them. One was jammed with business suits spanning more than fifty years in style and reeking strongly of mothballs and dust. A dozen pairs of shoes stood in line on the hardwood floor.

In the other closet clothes shared the space with several cardboard boxes. At the pinnacle of the pile sat a shoe box. Neatly lettered on its side, in a style he recognized as Archie's, was Autobio/Archie J.

There were two rows of tape cassettes, orange-bordered ones, white-bordered ones, lined up in the box. Seventeen in all. Reading the label on one of the cassettes, he saw Chicago Years/Dictated 13 Jan. Each tape was dated and placed in sequence. The earliest went back a little more than two years, the most recent was dated 25 April. That was five days before Barney had met Beth and her father at the Newspaper Artists Guild banquet and been invited to try out for the ghosting job.

After shaking the box gently, he popped the lid back on. His knuckles brushed something as he set the box back. Another cassette had been under it.

This one was labeled Early New York (and Romances)/Dictated 11 Nov.

Why wasn't this one in the box?

He ticked it against his lower teeth, then returned the cassette to its hiding place under the autobiographical shoe box.

"Be silly to look under the bed."

He looked under the bed.

Nothing but dust, a crumpled tissue and a peppermint drop.

Barney located Beth's room, and that of her father. There was nothing in either to tell him where the missing cartoonist was.

Beth had told him the mansion had an enormous multiroomed basement. That would be a good place to hide most anything.

Better hurry, though. Their banker may not be drunk today.

HE FELT THE PAST closing in on him before he left the last of the wooden steps. The first room of the basement was walled with bundles of old newspaper Sunday-comic sections. They rested on wide board-and-brick shelves, wrapped in big clear-plastic garbage bags. These must be newspaper copies of every "Poor Little Pearl" page from just about the start.

There were scrapbooks, too, each wrapped in plastic sheeting. Thick with publicity stories, photos, fan mail, souvenirs, a year to a book. Probably started by Archie's long-dead wife and then carried on by his son.

The cement floor gave off a cold glow. There was a strong scent of mouse droppings.

The next room was for the storage of suitcases and old toys. Spilling out of one big Bekins box were dolls—plastic ones, rag ones, rubber ones.

Here's who Beth used to sleep with.

Raggedy Ann, Barbie, some blonde he couldn't identify.

Atop a suitcase whose hide was spotted with travel stickers from the 1930s was a cardboard box. Scrawled across the lid, in a child's hand, was Valentines My Frends Have Send Me. Valentines from twenty years ago were stuffed into the box, many featuring forgotten TV cartoon characters. They all swore love and devotion to a little girl variously designated as Bith, Bethnee, Bethany, Beth and Best.

Hey, watch it. Don't get tearful.

Dropping the box, Barney pushed on to the next room.

He located the light switch on the wall of the third chill basement room. The single dangling bulb came alive, showing him an empty concrete-floored room.

No, not quite empty.

Leaning against one wall was an expensive Italian ten-speed bicycle. The front wheel was badly bent and twisted, broken spokes pronging out in several directions. There was mud caked on one pedal and on the seat, a small streak of mud on the chain. No mud on the rest of the frame, though, nor any trace of it in the treads of the tires.

"Okay, we've got his bike. Now where is Archie?"

Across the room he noticed now a thin line of yellow light along the floor.

There was a door there, masked by the shadows. The door was padlocked.

Why lock this and not the others?

He remembered seeing a tool chest on one of the shelves among the funny papers. He ran back through Beth's past and Archie's, fetched the chest.

Hunched over the padlock, he checked his watch and was surprised to find he'd already been prowling their house for nearly an hour. There was no time left for subtlety.

Selecting a large file, he used it as a lever to pry at the hasp of the lock. The cross-hatching of the file dug into his palm for minutes before he heard the satisfying snap of metal giving way.

He unhooked the remains of the padlock, dropped it to the floor and opened the door.

Discarded appliances were stored in the small square room. The unshaded sixty-watt bulb burned dimly in the low white ceiling. There was an old washer in the corner, a dishwasher and a large, low deep-freeze.

The freezer was immediately to the right of the doorway. There was a streak of mud traced across its white front. The thing was plugged in, throbbing and humming quietly.

Barney took a deep breath and yanked up the lid.

"Holy Christ!"

The search was over. Archie Judd was in there.

Wrapped in two clear plastic garbage bags. He looked like a man trapped under ice, face pressed desperately against it in search of air.

Barney made himself stay there looking into the dead man's face, forcing himself to take in the details. The left side of the old man's head was smashed, hollowed in by a deep wound. Blood had dried and caked black around the wound, making a distorted many-legged spider on the side of his blue-white face. Some of the blood had crawled across his cheek to clot alongside his flattened nose. There was mud all over him, splashed across the front of his clothes. Archie was dressed in faded khaki trousers, a much washed plaid flannel shirt and a heavy gray coat sweater with leather elbow patches, the kind of a sweater favored by old men who play chess in parks.

Barney lowered his free hand in, touching Archie Judd's body. The old man was frozen solid.

He was still holding up the freezer lid with his other hand when he heard the scraping on the floor just outside the doorway.

Beth appeared on the threshold. "I'm sorry you did this," she said. There was a .32 revolver in her hand.

14

THE GUN WAS AIMED at him.

Shaking his head sadly, Barney said, "So you did kill him, huh?"

"What?" Her eyebrows went up, then down. "Nobody killed him, what are you talking about?"

"He's sure as hell dead."

"There was an accident, when he was cycling. That was weeks ago, toward the end of April."

"Just before the banquet." He was still holding the lid of the freezer open, cold air was swirling around him. "Where'd you find Archie?"

"My father did. On the road up behind the estate, the road he always cycled along," she answered. "He was down at the bottom of a little gully, his head had hit a tree trunk and it was. . . like that. His bike was all banged up, next to him on the ground."

Barney let the lid drop. It made an unsettling thump sound. "The bicycle I saw in the next room, that's Archie's?"

"I thought you were a prowler when I heard you from upstairs. That's how come I brought this." She lowered the revolver. "What do you mean about the bike? Sure, it was grandfather's."

"Did someone clean it up afterward?"

"No, we simply brought everything here," she said. "We left everything. . .even grandfather. . .just as it was."

He leaned his backside against the low freezer, realized what was inside and straightened up. "Your notion is Archie somehow lost control of his bike, went skidding off the road and down a hillside, is that it? He crashed his bike into a tree trunk and smashed his head."

"Well, yes." She was puzzled. "I mean, there he was against the tree and there was his bike all mangled. What else could we think?"

"I did some illustrations for a magazine once, a guided-tour-of-the-morgue sort of piece," Barney said. "I picked up a few things, and I don't think the wound on Archie's head was made by hitting a tree."

"What did he hit then?"

"No, something hit him," he told her. "Was it raining that day, the morning you found his body?"

She shook her head. "No, though it had the day before. The hillside was pretty muddy, we got splashed. . .getting him away from there. Fortunately hardly anyone uses that road anymore."

"The road's paved." He knew it was since he had his car hidden just off it. "So all the mud on Archie got on him after he left the road."

"That's what I've been saying."

"Yes, but there's hardly any mud at all on his bicycle. C'mon, we'll take another look." He edged by her and her dangling revolver into the other room.

Switching the gun to her left hand, Beth knelt to trace a finger along the bicycle frame. "There isn't much mud dried on here at all, is there?"

"If he'd gone careering down the hill, there'd be a lot more on the tires, the derailleur, the chain wheel, the front fork, everywhere."

"I can never remember the names of all the parts."

"I illustrated a bicycle catalog once, when I was starting out." He pointed at the bike. "Even if this thing had gone sliding down the hill on its side, it would have collected a lot more dirt on its carcass."

She straightened up, shifting the gun back to her right hand. "But there's mud all over grand-father."

"From lying facedown at the bottom of your gully," he said. "I think somebody carried him down the hillside after bashing in his skull with a heavy rock or a hunk of pipe. They arranged him against the tree trunk, where your father found him. Obviously you didn't check for foot-prints around there?"

"By the time I saw the scene," she said slowly, "dad had been up and down the hillside a couple of times. We weren't thinking about anything but an accident."

"Whoever did it was no doubt smart enough to wipe out most of the traces of himself anyway," Barney said. "For all he could predict the cops might be the first ones to the body. After he left Archie's body down there, he climbed back up the hill, probably getting rid of his footprints as he went. Then he gave the front wheel a few good whacks with his blunt instrument, picked it up and tossed it down to rest next to Archie. Old people have falling-down accidents all the time; if the killer was lucky nobody would suspect it was anything else."

Beth touched his arm hesitantly. "I can't believe he was murdered."

"Well, he damn well was," he said. "Now suppose you tell me why he's on ice and why the hell you haven't told anyone about this?"

THE ICE CUBES in Russell Judd's glass wouldn't stop rattling. He set it, using both hands, on the coffee table before him. "We had a very simple and basic reason, Barney," he said. "Money."

Beth was sitting on the living-room sofa beside Barney, not quite touching him. "The minute Archie Judd dies, everything stops," she said. " 'Poor Little Pearl' becomes the property of Independent Features. Every penny it earns goes to the syndicate and my father and I are left with nothing."

"Wouldn't they keep you on, Russ?" he asked. "You've been managing and writing the strip for years."

"On the books I'm listed as earning a salary of forty thousand dollars a year for my work on 'Pearl.'" Judd reached for his glass, decided against it. "That money came to me from my father. Our relationship with Langendorf and the other syndicate executives has always been cordial, but I never kidded myself into thinking they have any affection toward me or Beth. Even for Archie for that matter."

Beth picked up. "To keep dad on the feature they'd be obliged to pay him roughly as much as Archie did," she said. "Something around forty thousand a year. Suppose, though, they bring in a new team to produce 'Pearl'? Archie was well-known, but not a celebrity like Al Capp or Charlie Schulz. The public'll buy 'Pearl' just as readily without the Judd name on it. That little waif is the one who's the valuable property, not any of us. Okay, so Langendorf hires a new team. You know damn well they can get a good artist for six hundred dollars a week, or maybe less. There are plenty of writers who'd take the scripting job for a hundred and fifty or two hundred and fifty dollars a week. So figure it out. For around forty thousand dollars or less they

can get the whole package, writing *and* drawing. My father's arrangement was with Archie,
not the syndicate. They might let him stay on,
but we weren't ready to gamble on it.''

''The syndicates aren't that much different,
ours anyway, than the people at Maximus,''
said Judd. ''They're not sentimental.''

''There is one thing that occurs to me,''
Barney told them. ''This strip's been earning
more than half a million a year for years, I hear.
You folks live in a very expensive, albeit
gloomy, mansion. So even if the syndicate cuts
you off the minute they learn the news, you've
still got this estate and would inherit quite a—''

''There's just about nothing to inherit,'' said
Beth.

''C'mon, don't try to—''

''Archie only allowed me to handle the business aspects of the strip,'' explained Judd.
''The actual money that came in, he kept control of. We had quite a few battles, since I was
always in favor of investing the considerable
profits from 'Pearl' in real estate, tax-free
bonds and government notes. Archie, in his last
years, craved something more exciting. He
stopped living up to his reputation for being
tight with a dollar. I'm afraid he became con-
vinced he was a stock-market wizard.''

''He wasn't, though, and lost nearly two million dollars in the past three years,'' said Beth
quietly. ''Right now dad and I have about one

hundred thousand dollars in savings. The total Archie Judd estate, excluding this house, amounts to less than thirteen thousand."

"Thanks to Archie's speculations there's still a fantastic mortgage on this house," added Judd. "Not to mention a crippling property tax."

Barney glanced from Beth's profile to the pale face of her father. "Okay, I understand your motive more or less," he said. "You convince everyone Archie is still alive and the money keeps pouring in."

"I'm aware that someone with a hundred thousand in the bank ought not to complain," said Judd. "Yet I feel we deserve a damn lot more. My father *created* this strip, it was his idea and no one else's. I've worked on it since I left the service in my twenties. 'Poor Little Pearl' is ours, we started it. But, because of the nature of the newspaper-syndication business, it's next to impossible for any artist to own his feature. It simply isn't fair and so we decided to do something about it."

"But how long did you figure to bring this off? Sooner or later—"

"We only need a year or two," said Beth. "The profits, our share of them, from the musical and the TV show ought to add up to a million or more. With that safely invested, dad would be taken care of comfortably for the rest of his life."

"You've been signing his name on the strips," he said to Judd, "and on the checks, too, I imagine."

"I do a near-perfect Archie Judd signature."

"Your family doctor has to be in on this."

"Dr. Emerson was very close to Archie and he happens to share our feelings about the situation," said Judd. "I knew I could trust him to cooperate."

"You were figuring to wait a year, then have Dr. Emerson write a death certificate?"

"Yes," said Beth. "For years grandfather rarely left the house. That trip to the Graphics Art Museum was one of the few exceptions in a long while. He's old, he's got a reputation for being a recluse, and a feisty one to boot."

"Suppose someone dropped in unexpectedly, wanted to see him?"

"We'd say he was sick and couldn't have visitors," she replied. "Besides which, none of the syndicate people have ever been to the house and they're not likely to start popping by now. So long as the work comes in on time every week, they don't care how he is."

Leaving the sofa he wandered to a window. The day was fading away. It seemed awfully early for that, but a check of his wristwatch showed it wasn't. "You picked me to ghost because I didn't know him and had never met him," he said with his back to them. "I was easier to fool."

"You were the best artist," Judd said.

"Sure, but if Jape Easter had been coming here regularly, you might not have been able to con him with the cassette business," he said. "And a glad-hander like Jocko Pease would be inclined to go barging right upstairs to tell Archie a couple jokes to cheer him up."

Beth asked, "You knew about the tapes?"

"Yeah." He turned to face her.

"For how long?"

"Since before Boston."

She smoothed her dark skirt. "Why didn't you say something?"

"Several reasons. I didn't know then what had actually happened to him," he said. "Is that really his voice on the tapes, taken from his audio memoirs?"

"Mostly it's me," said Judd. "Someone yells and bullies you for half a century, you become quite good at mimicking his voice and inflections. I did use those autobiographic tapes of his to make sure my impersonation was right."

"You could just as well have done Bugs Bunny," he told Beth's father. "Since I never heard the real Archie."

"I wanted it to be right, to have the details ring true. We didn't know who else besides you we might have to work it on either." Judd gathered up his drink, was more successful at keeping it from jiggling. "We assumed that if we could give you the impression Archie was up in bed being his usual nasty self, you'd put that information on the Fairfield County grapevine. All the local cartoonists would eventually know and it would filter on into Manhattan and the syndicate."

"I was playing what the old B-movie private eyes call the patsy," Barney said, mostly toward the girl.

"I didn't like doing this to you," she said, avoiding his glance. "We had to do something, though."

"Well, hell, long as you feel bad about making a fool of me, I won't be offended. Okay?"

"It doesn't make much difference now," said Judd with a weak sigh. "We're all through, since you've found out our secret."

Barney returned to the sofa. "You have another problem, Russ," he said. "Somebody murdered Archie and they must've had a reason."

"You suggested that before, yet I can't believe—"

"Damn it, trust me," cut in Barney. "He did not injure his head in any fall from a bike. Someone very deliberately smashed in his skull with a blunt instrument. Crashing into a tree trunk simply wouldn't produce a—"

"Barney, you don't believe father and I—"

"Let's not put that to a test just yet," he said. "You are sitting here telling me, oh, we gathered grandfather up like so much garbage, we stuffed him in a freezer in the basement, bribed a doctor to tell a whole stewpot of lies. But, jimmyjams, we aren't killers or anything bad like that. Shucks, we did all this for a noble reason. Greed."

She made a strange sound in her throat and swung out to slap him hard across the cheek. "Who the hell are you to act so damn smug? What's so honest and courageous about what you're doing? You go whining around about your true calling, about being a great artist. Yet you spend your life drawing crap for Maximus and ghosting for us. What's your excuse? Oh, you need the money. Well, welcome to the club. That's exactly why we did what we did. And we got a hell of a bigger payoff than you."

He was breathing carefully in and out. "Maybe so, but I never pretended to be in love with someone just to keep him from finding out my grandfather was—"

"I wasn't pretending, you jerk! I do love you."

Judd coughed into his hand. "Maybe we ought to get back to what you mean to do next, Barney," he said. "I realize you have very little reason to trust us, but I really can assure you that until less than an hour ago I believed Archie had died in a simple accident."

Forcing himself to concentrate on Judd and edit out as much of Beth's presence as he could, Barney went over again what he had told the girl about the circumstances of the old man's death. "Could be I'm wrong," he wound up. "But I don't think this was any accident."

"I can't think of anyone with a reason for killing him." Judd leaned back in his chair. "He made a lot of enemies in his life, but managed to outlive just about all of them."

"Even so, somebody did murder him," said Barney. "That person had a motive, a good reason. He has to be wondering why his murder didn't take, because for all he knows Archie is still alive. If his motive is strong enough, he's going to try again."

Beth asked, "Do you think this prowler you've seen might be the one?"

"Might be. It must be frustrating to kill someone and then have it turn out maybe you didn't," Barney said. "He's got to be worried about what shape the old man is in, why he hasn't blown the whistle on him."

"The other night, though, that was Jape," said the girl. "He can't be the—"

"Jape Easter claims that was his first offense as a lurker. If he's telling the truth, then we may have two different prowlers. At this point I don't know whether I believe Jape or not."

Judd drank down a good half of his Scotch and soda. "What do you propose to do now, Barney?" he asked. "Report us to the police?"

"If I do that right now, the law may just pin the killing on you two," he answered. "Or at least charge you both with being accessories to the murder. I, despite what Beth may think of my character, don't want that to happen.''

Judd said, ''What's the alternative?''

''We can't bring the police in until we can tell them exactly who it was who killed Archie and why.''

''How do we learn that?''

''We start digging,'' Barney said. ''See, there's one more thing to worry about. The killer may have a reason for wanting all three of you dead, not just Archie.''

''I can't believe that,'' said Beth.

Her father said, ''You'll keep on working for us, Barney? Continue to ghost 'Pearl'?''

He stood. ''Until the murder's solved,'' he promised.

15

THE OLD CARTOONIST'S BEDROOM felt chill; the gray of the midmorning seemed to be trying to push in at the windows. Barney placed the shoe box of autobiographical tapes atop the bedside table next to the cassette player. In his other hand he held the tape Archie Judd had kept separate.

He sat gingerly on the edge of the dead man's bed. Somewhere in these damn tapes, in this one especially, might be a clue about why the old man had been murdered. A clue, Barney was hoping, that would point away from Beth and her father.

"Let's give a listen." He fit the cassette into the machine.

The last time Archie's voice had come out of these speakers Beth and her dad had been trying to con him. But that was over now, everyone was being open.

He wanted very much to believe that.

After a couple of deep breaths, he pressed down the play button.

Archie Judd said, "She was really something, a thoroughgoing bitch but a joy to behold. A star then, though nobody much remembers her now. It was when I had the studio on East Thirty-second and she was starring in *Apple Blossoms* at the Hunneker Theater on Broadway. Well, sir, by the time I got the idea of sort of commemorating our little relationship in the strip, Irene Loftin and me weren't exactly as close as we had been. Dumb thing to do anyhow, since I was supposed to be a happily married man with a wife and a young son up in Connecticut. Couldn't resist, though, and so I put something into a Sunday page. Had Pearl and her mangy cat stop in an alley to stare up at a poster advertisng Irene in her damn play. Pearl says something cute like, 'Jimmyjams, wouldn't it be swell if I grew up to look like that, Muffin?' I got right on the syndicate, twisted Langendorf's arm...that was the old man, father of the current sap who heads Independent...and got me the original back right after the engravers had finished mangling it. Had to rush, like a nut, right over to Irene's apartment. She was living in a very impressive joint over on Central Park West. Anyway, I hand her the drawing and give her a spiel about how we ought to keep being friends. Well, that bitch curses me up one side and down the other, then she grabs the damn drawing and rips it clean in two. Yes sir, she ripped it in halves and then in quarters and then into eighths. Flings the whole shooting match right in my puss, and in those days I was using four-ply bristol board. Getting a flurry of that smack in the kisser didn't cheer me up none. She told me that sleeping with me now and then hadn't been all that terrible, but if I thought I could start bragging about it in print, why—''

''Finding anything?''

Barney pushed the stop button on the cassette player. He looked across at Beth, who was standing in the doorway of the old cartoonist's bedroom. ''You're talking to me again?''

''Yes, I'm sorry I swung on you last evening.'' She moved into the room and sat on the edge of the bed beside him. ''Since you're going to be poking around the house for a while, we may as well be friends again.''

''Okay, good.''

''Are you getting anything helpful out of those autobiography tapes of grandfather's?''

Barney tapped the machine on the bedside table. ''I'm starting with the one he'd pulled from the box and left separate,'' he told her. ''Not getting much, although I have a nagging feeling I ought to be.''

''Archie fooled around quite a bit,'' she said. ''I hadn't realized.''

''He didn't mention anything about why this particular tape was kept separate?''

Beth shook her head. ''Barney, I never paid

all that much attention to this life-story project of his," she said. "It all got going when somebody, *Cartoonists Profiles* maybe, asked him for a couple pages of background stuff on his life and career. Archie decided to dictate it. Once he got rolling he simply kept babbling. If you go through all those tapes you'll probably develop a good case of boredom."

"Some of the stuff is interesting. Archie was a close friend and drinking buddy of Tad Dorgan, for instance. Most of those anecdotes are interesting."

"Who was Tad Dorgan?"

"Just another dead cartoonist."

"I came up to ask you something," she said. "Do you want to have lunch with me here? I'll fix you something if you do."

"That'll be fine."

"One more thing. Could you possibly play escort for me this coming weekend?"

"Where to this time?"

"The Newspaper Artists Guild boating party. You know, they're renting some sort of old ferryboat, complete with dixieland band, and sailing around the Sound on Saturday night."

"I thought you and Russ were going to attend that."

"Dad has to go down to Philadelphia instead. They're having problems with the book of the 'Poor Little Pearl' musical and are apparently so desperate they're willing to consult the man who actually writes the strip. So dad isn't going to be around Saturday.''

"Sea voyages are supposed to be good for you," he said. "I accept."

"It's going to be a challenge to both of us," Beth said. "Langendorf and most of the other top syndicate executives will be along."

"I can fake them out," he said. "Lying to editors and publishers is something I've had experience with."

"You shouldn't be involved in this mess at all. If only you hadn't been so damn curious."

"Yeah, that's what they told Pandora." He took her hand. "My motive was more than just curiosity. It was important to find out what happened to Archie."

"Because you thought maybe I'd done him harm?"

"I knew something was going on wrong. People were prowling around, Archie was missing," he said. "Look, I'm not going to apologize for being concerned about you."

"You don't have to. It's just that things are so tangled up. I've been trying to make sure dad doesn't lose the strip or all the money, trying to hold onto you and yet not confide anything. And nothing is getting any clearer or easier. This is like a disease that keeps spreading and spreading."

"We'll clear things up," he said. "Soon, too."

16

"CAN YOU CATCH THE PHONE?" Beth asked. She was holding one of her shoes, rubbing at its toe with a moistened tissue.

Barney arose from the butterfly chair he'd been slouched in, crossed to the phone on the table near the girl's bed. "Good evening, Judd residence."

A few seconds of heavy breathing.

"Hello. Who the hell is this?"

A click followed by the dial tone murmuring in his ear.

"Who was it?" asked Beth as he hung up.

"He didn't say." Barney stayed beside the table, watching her as she slipped the shoe on.

"Was it some kind of crank—"

"Only a wrong number. That's a splendid dress."

"It's only my basic black cocktail dress," she said, smiling. "Wait'll I add the string of pearls and then the uniform'll be complete."

"Okay, but on you it's far from a cliché."

"Thanks, I didn't mean to sound—"

The phone rang again and Barney snatched up the receiver. "Yeah?" he said loudly.

"Barney, this is Russ Judd," came the voice of Beth's father. "You sound a bit upset. Is everything all right up there?"

"Yes, it is, Russ. Must be the excitement about this boat trip tonight you hear in my voice. You still down in Philadelphia?"

"Unfortunately, yes."

"Is Bethany handy?"

"Right here, loading herself down with baubles. I'll—"

"Let me say something to you first."

"Sure, go ahead, Russ."

"You'll be running into all sorts of people on this little jaunt around the Sound, Barney. Some who've been friends of Archie's for years, as well as syndicate executives who're very much interested in the current state of his health."

"I realize that."

"I'm sure you do. I merely want to add my own word of appreciation," Judd said. "We, both of us, appreciate what you've been doing to help out. Be careful tonight, keep an eye on Bethany."

"I intend to."

"If she's there, I'd like to speak to her."

"Sure." Barney held the receiver out toward the girl. "Your dad."

"So I gathered." She had both hands behind

her neck, fastening the string of pearls. When she took the phone from him, she kissed him on the cheek before speaking into the receiver. "Hi, dad. How much longer are you going to be stuck...."

Barney returned to the canvas chair.

Russell Judd hadn't much to say apparently, because Beth hung up after only a few minutes of conversation.

Judd had certainly come across clearly, not as though he were talking on a long distance hook-up at all.

Suppose he wasn't actually in Philadelphia? Suppose for some reason they only wanted Barney to believe....

He stood up, rubbing the heel of his hand over one temple. He had to get this whole damn thing straightened out soon. He didn't seem capable of trusting anyone, anymore.

"...fashionably late," Beth was saying to him.

"Hmm?"

"I was telling you I would rather arrive at parties unfashionably early than fashionably late," Beth said, frowning across the bedroom at him. "Especially when the party is on a boat, which might sail without us. Want to leave now?"

"Yeah, let's go."

"I appreciate all you—"

"Your dad already gave me a testimonial."
Barney took her hand. "I didn't tell him this,
but you ought to know I'm here because I'm in
love with you."

She nodded once. "I know, yes."

A FEW MINUTES away from the dock the fog
began to close in on the brightly lighted ferryboat. Thin at this stage, the fog only blurred the
lights of the Connecticut shore and hazed the
night sky. Out in the open on the main deck a
six-piece band, each member in straw hat and
candy-stripe blazer, was blasting out dixieland.
The central salon, which contained the largest
bar, was clogged with people. The deck was
crowded, too.

"What are the symptoms of seasickness?"
Barney asked Beth.

The two of them were at the port railing
watching the shore fade away into the growing
fog. The girl had her arm linked with his.

She asked, "You feeling odd?"

"There's a sort of contraction in my chest
and—"

"Maybe your underwear's shrunk."

He cocked an eyebrow. "You're in a pretty
whimsical mood tonight."

"It is all an act, believe me. Inside I'm as
gloomy as ever," Beth said. "I didn't mean to
kid you about feeling ill."

"Not exactly ill. If I wasn't a skeptic, I'd say I

was suffering from a premonition. Feel like something nasty is coming up."

"Sticking with father and me is making you jittery. You really ought—"

"It's you I'm sticking with," he said. "And let's change the subject."

"Did you ever—speaking of ships and the sea—sail to Europe?"

"Nope."

"When I was eighteen dad and I took the. . . oops, yonder comes Langendorf."

"President of your syndicate?"

"That very Langendorf, yep," she answered. "Good evening, Mr. Langendorf."

The stocky, gray-haired man put an arm around the girl, kissed her wetly on the cheek. "Always a pleasure to see you, Bethany," he said. "Where are Archie and Russ?"

"Grandfather's home with his baby-sitter, still too under the weather for a sea cruise," she said. "Dad is in Philadelphia acting as play doctor for the 'Pearl' musical."

"Don't envy Russ," said the syndicate head with a mock shudder. "Philly is not a town to linger in. It is exactly what W.C. Fields said it was, or was he talking about Pittsburgh? You must be Bernie Kains."

"Barney Kains," he corrected.

"Never could figure out how you people decide which Bernard will be Bernie and which Barney."

"We have a special group of fanatical Zionist commandos who do that." Barney extended his hand. "Pleased to meet you, sir."

The older man's grip was firm. "You're doing one heck of a fine job helping Archie out on 'Poor Little Pearl.'"

"He's doing a marvelous job," Beth put in.

"Would you mind, dear, if I had a small private talk with our young friend? There are a couple things I want to discuss now I have him trapped on the same boat with me." Langendorf chuckled, taking his arm away from the girl's shoulders.

"I'll be in the salon, Barney."

"No, Beth, I don't think we ought to—"

"Don't worry, you talk business." She turned, went walking away through the people on the deck.

Barney started after her, the syndicate president's arm blocked him. "I really should—"

"Plenty of time for romance, Barney. The night's still young, this won't take long," Langendorf assured him. "You have a very good reputation in the field."

He lost sight of the girl. "Hmm?"

"She is damned attractive, isn't she? If you like them on the skinny side. I never could figure out how someone who got part of her genes from Archie Judd could turn out so well." Langendorf chuckled once more. "We think 'Poor Little Pearl' has been looking considerably better since you started ghosting it. In fact—"

"I'm not actually ghosting, only assisting."

"You can save the bullshit for the fans. I'm sure, from what I hear, that Archie isn't in any shape to do much on the strip right now," he said. "I didn't want to bring this up in front of Bethany, but we'd like to put the old boy out to pasture fairly soon. Fifty years is long enough to draw a strip."

He's already about as out to pasture as you can get. "I don't think Archie's quite ready to quit," Barney lied.

"We're not heartless up at Independent." Langendorf rested a stubby elbow on the white railing. "I'm not suggesting we toss Archie out like so much garbage simply because he's senile."

He's sure wrapped for it. Barney shook his head, trying to clear it of the image of Archie Judd shrouded in garbage bags. "What exactly are you suggesting, sir?"

"We want Archie to seriously consider the idea of stepping down. He can phase himself out, let's say, in the next year," said Langendorf. "After that, you can officially take over, Barney. At which time we'd, dealing directly with you, be willing to pay you one thousand dollars."

"Per week?"

"Obviously."

"I appreciate the offer, sir, except right at the moment I'm—"

"We're not exactly speaking of right this minute. You only have to think about what I've said, roll it around in your mind for a while."

"How exactly do you plan to phase him out? Would Archie still pull in half the profits from—"

"No, that wouldn't be feasible. We'd have to settle on a generous pension figure. One that everyone involved could live with. It would be, of course, much less than he's dragging down now."

"You think Archie and the rest of the family would sit still for—"

"You've so far been hearing only the Judd side of this issue. Granted, Archie did invent 'Poor Little Pearl.' I'm the first to admit that my late father had nothing to do with it. He wasn't like Captain Patterson at the *News* syndicate, he never had a creative part in any of the Independent features." He swung around to stare directly at Barney. "What we do, though, is sell the bejesus out of our features. Do you know that 'Pearl' is still picking up newspapers? That's how we make money in this business, by adding client papers. Some of the hick-town sheets pay as little as ten bucks a week for a strip, but if you can get five hundred papers like that on your client list, that's five thousand dollars coming in every week." Langendorf paused, catching his breath. "We've got the best staff of salesmen in the country, better than King, better than United. Archie Judd has lived the very soft life all these years because our sales force has been on the road busting its balls for 'Poor Little Pearl.'"

"He does provide you with a salable product, though."

"Granted, though I sometimes think we could sell just about anything." He gave Barney's nearest arm a light punch. "Well, there are all sorts of people on this cruise I have to talk to. Keep in mind what I'm offering you, Barney. Call me in New York sometime soon and we'll have lunch."

Barney had the impression he might be expected to salute now. "Yes, I'll remember all this," he said carefully.

Another punch. "Very good." Langendorf did a smooth about-face and went striding across the deck.

"You didn't sell it, did you?"

Barney spun, saw Texaco grinning at him from beside a life preserver that had *Greenwich Queen* stenciled on it. "Sell what?"

"Your soul." The curly-headed little cartoonist came closer. "I was waiting for Langendorf to produce the parchment and the smoking ink."

"No souls changed hands. And you have to

admit he's a few notches more amiable than
Carlotsky.''

"So was Jack the Ripper." Putting his elbows
on the rail, he gazed into the burgeoning fog. "I
only caught the tag end of the Temptation of
Barney Kains. What'd he offer?''

"Thousand a week to take over 'Pearl.' ''

"That's almost twice as good as six hundred,
amigo.''

"All I have to do is help him dump Archie
Judd, Beth and her father from the strip.''

"I thought, from the way the guy was cluck-
ing, you were going to have to do something
bad.''

Barney said, "I didn't know you were going to
attend this affair tonight.''

"Once again I am freeloading,'' his friend explained. "Carlotsky decided at the last minute
that he couldn't sail due to his having to go see
Warloff in Bellevue.''

"Wait now, Carlotsky is actually going to visit
a sick artist? That sounds—''

"Before he went stark raving nutso, Warloff
hid eleven finished pages of 'Peter Pupp' someplace around the bull pen. Carlotsky, aided by
most of us, cannot find 'em. The stuff is due at
the engraver no later than next Tuesday, so Big
C hopes to pry the hiding place out of poor old
Warloff. He was reading up on truth serum and
electroshock before he departed.''

"Well, welcome aboard,'' he said. "Have you

seen Beth? She drifted off when Langendorf descended on us.''

"I noticed her in the bar few minutes back," said Texaco, "with a chap closely resembling Jape Easter.''

"Jape Easter? What the hell is he—''

"Don't consider him fit company?''

"I better go find her.''

"Mayhap you can give me a little information before you dash off. I spotted a lass on the upper deck who is an absolutely uncanny double for the late Inger Stevens. Would you have any idea who she might be?''

"I'm not even exactly sure who Inger Stevens was." Barney noticed his feet were impatiently pawing at the deck. "I'll get back to you after I locate Beth, okay?''

"Go with my blessings.''

The fog was much thicker now, surrounding the slow, chuffing ferryboat, climbing over the railings. Barney nodded greetings at several Newspaper Artists Guild members as he elbowed his way toward the salon.

"Barney Kains. Listen, you have to hear this." Jocko Pease, clutching a plastic martini glass, planted his shaggy form in his path. "Stan Drake just told me this one. Seems this rabbi is lost in the desert with—''

"Already heard it, Jocko." He edged around the big man.

"Funny as hell, isn't it?''

"Funny." He hurried along, the salon doors still yards off.

Beth shouldn't be with Jape Easter. He'd been lurking around the mansion, he might even—

The polished oaken doors of the salon snapped open and a tall red-haired woman stepped out into the misty night. She recognized the approaching Barney, threw her lovely arms wide and cried out, "Darling!"

It was Tawny.

17

THE IMAGE of his onetime wife seemed to burn through the fog, the blazing red hair, the shimmering emerald disco gown, the glistening crimson-lipped smile.

Nothing.

Barney smiled as he realized he wasn't feeling any exceptional reaction. No elevated pulse, no ringing in the ears, not a single palpitation. Nary a trace of the old lust, nothing of fright.

"Evening, Tawny," he was able to say in his regular, everyday voice.

Tawny put her palms together under her lovely chin in that Shirley-Temple-praying-for-her-sick-puppy gesture of hers, inhaled in that swallowing-laughter way and said, "You're looking well, Barney."

"You, too."

Cured.

He was completely cured, like the reformed drunk who could walk by his favorite saloon without having his feet trot him on inside, like the former addict who could spend a night in a pharmacy and not feel the slightest itch to shoot, sniff, pop or smoke anything. It was absolutely terrific. He wished he had a crutch he could fling away to commemorate this miracle.

"Um, listen," said the woman he used to sleep with, "I'm a guest of the Langendorfs tonight, Barn. I, um, was really hoping I'd bump into you."

He nodded. "I'm in somewhat of a hurr—"

"See, we're on the verge of signing a very nice contract," Tawny went on in that breathless way of hers. "I'm going to be doing a beauty column for Independent Features. Isn't that neat?"

"Neat. Now I—"

"I understand you're very close with the Judd family, tight," Tawny said. "They have a real lot of clout with Independent. So, for old times' sake, um, it'd be nice if you urged them to put in a nice word with Langendorf for me. I think the deal's set already but it couldn't hurt, huh?"

"Be glad to, Tawny. In fact, I'm on my way to meet one of the Judds right now."

"Um, thanks." She aimed a grateful kiss at his cheek.

Barney dodged, made it to the doorway of the salon. "Nice running into you again."

"I'll, um, need pictures to go with my column. You could draw them maybe."

"Something to think about." He pushed into the salon.

Ty Banner waved from the corner where he was huddled with his wife and several of the Inkwell Restaurant regulars. Someone he was fairly certain was John Norment was seated atop the bar and singing sentimental songs. Barney made a circuit of the packed room and found no trace of Beth. He struggled out of there and decided to check the upper deck.

At the foot of the metal stairway leading up he encountered Bud Heinz.

"Hi, I'm Bud Heinz," said the lanky gray-haired cartoonist. "We more or less met up in Boston."

"Shared that memorable panel, yes." Barney shook his hand. "Never did get around to mentioning how much I like your 'Seaweed Sam' strip, Bud."

"Been doing it for thirty-six years, but I still get a boot out of hearing someone say that," said Heinz. "You appear to be, if I may say so, pretty darn euphoric. Are you drinking something I ought to know about?"

"Nothing like that," said Barney, grinning. "I'm this way because I've just enjoyed a complete and total remission."

"I hadn't heard you were sick."

"I just realized it myself. Now, if you'll excuse me, Bud, I'm looking for someone."

"We all are, though most of us never find the. . . ."

He bumped into Mort Walker as he went rushing up the stairs. "Hello, Mort."

"Hi, Barney."

The fog had taken over the upper deck, rubbing out the details of the cabins, railings and even most of the deck.

Barney stumbled over a plastic cocktail glass, which sent the dregs of two ice cubes skating across the deck and off into the unseen night sea.

A hand shot out of the fog to take hold of his arm.

"Good to see you again, Barney."

He made out the plump beaming shape of Willis Folger. "I keep running into my Boston con buddies," Barney said.

"Never really had much of a chance to talk to you up there," said Folger. "You probably think of me as a plain and simple cartoon nut, but I do a lot more besides collect. For one thing, I do a fair amount of selling, too."

"Selling originals?"

"Right, and I've got several customers who'd love one of your Human Beast pages," Folger continued. "Maximus is supposed to return those to you, aren't they?"

"Never thought to ask. I suppose so."

"If you'd let me handle your stuff exclusively, I can offer you twenty bucks a page, thirty

for splash pages," said the plump young man.
"That may not sound like much, but it comes to
three hundred and fifty dollars for each complete story. You might not know it, but some of
your fellow Maximus artists aren't worth more
than ten or fifteen bucks a page retail."

"Well, next time I'm up at the offices, I'll see
if I can swipe a bundle of my originals then."

Smiling, Folger produced a business card.
"Give me a call. We pick up and deliver," he
said. "I'll pay you in front, too, even before I
sell the stuff. I guess I'll head down to—"

"Something I wanted to check with you."
Barney slid the card into his sport-coat pocket.

"Any sort of original you might want for
yourself I can—"

"What I want is some information. About the
visit you and Archie Judd made to the Graphic
Arts Museum."

Folger lowered his head. "I really feel badly
about that, Barney," he said. "He fell sick
shortly after the trip and I'm sure Bethany and
her father blame me. I swear, though, Archie
was in good shape that day. It really upset me
when I heard he was down with something fairly serious."

"What Archie's got has nothing to do with
you," Barney assured him. "Did anything
unusual happen while you were there with
him?"

"Such as what?"

"I don't know exactly, something odd. Something that might have unsettled Archie." Barney was fishing, with no very clear idea of what he hoped to land.

"Let's see." Folger was thoughtful, remembering. "We looked at the originals, the collection Jocko had stored in the warehouse. Archie did do sort of a take when he saw one of the three Sunday pages of 'Poor Little Pearl' Jocko had bought in that big collection."

"How'd he react exactly?"

"He muttered something like, 'Never thought I'd see this again.' When I asked him what he meant, he wouldn't answer me," said Folger. "Later, though, when we were taking those pictures, Archie made sure I took a couple of him and that particular drawing."

"We have a set of those photos, but...." Barney thought he heard something off in the fog. He narrowed his eyes, spotted nothing. "I don't remember which drawing is in the photo."

"It's from that sequence in 1930 when Pearl and Muffin, believing Uncle Goodworx was killed in the ocean-liner disaster, come to New York City to seek a new life. Anyway, she and the cat are wandering the streets and they notice a poster advertising *Apple Blossoms* with Irene Loftin, who was a big Broadway actress way back then. Pearl says, 'Jimmyjams, ain't she pretty, though, Muffin? Gollygosh, if I could only grow up to be half that beautiful!' Made a cute little interlude, and I have a hunch Archie was maybe fooling around with Irene Loftin, though I haven't as yet had the nerve to ask him.''

Holy Christ! That had to be what this was all about. ''The collection of originals, all the stuff that burned up,'' he said slowly. ''Where'd Jocko get it?''

Folger gave a rueful laugh. ''He pulled off a real coup there, Jocko did. The collection, several hundred choice pieces, belonged to one of the real pioneer comic-art collectors, a Colonel James Hobart Coulthard of Monroe, Ohio. He died, oh, twenty years ago and most people thought his whole collection was lost. Then Jocko, the sly bastard, succeeded in tracing down the widow. Turns out she'd kept the whole thing piled up in her barn. A lot of the drawings, including a beautiful early 'Terry And The Pirates' Sunday page, were rat-nibbled around the edges. Even so, if Jocko could have gotten them all cleaned up and framed, he would have had one of the most fantastic collections around. Not in terms of quantity, but for the rare pieces. My own damn fault for not trying to track down that old lady myself.''

Barney said, ''Jocko mentioned insuring the collection for something like half a million dollars. How was that figure arrived at?''

''Actually the collection's worth closer to

three-quarters of a million. *Was* since it's gone now," said Folger. "I ought to know its value, since I appraised all the material for Jocko and that list was what was used to get his insurance. I'm considered an expert, done this for several collectors and some estates."

"You're an expert on everything from 1900 on?"

Folger laughed. "Well, my own favorite era is the 1940s and 1950s, but I know enough about what a Herriman or a Winsor McKay is worth to be able to set a price," he said. "Despite people coming into this market to get themselves hedges against inflation or recession, there aren't all that many real experts around."

"Must've taken you a long time to go through all that artwork."

Folger said, "I did it all in one afternoon. As a cartoon nut I'd have liked to wallow in the stuff for a week, but Jocko and his insurance people were anxious to get it all itemized and evaluated. I whizzed through the job in about five hours."

"Meaning you didn't have time to examine each and every drawing carefully?"

Folger hesitated, frowning. "What are you getting at?"

"Just wondering if you'd had a chance to study the other drawings of Archie's," he said. "Nothing important. Have you seen Beth, by the way?"

"Didn't even know she was on board."

"We're supposed to be together, except I misplaced her."

"I'll tell her if I run into her," said Folger. "You will call me about your Maximus originals, won't you?"

"It's a deal." Barney left him to move along the upper deck.

The fog closed in tight around him, feeling spiky in his lungs when he inhaled. Groping, he touched the railing and paused to lean on it. Gazing out at what ought to be the night waters of the Long Island Sound, he reviewed what Folger had been saying to him.

It was obvious now what Archie had seen when—

An incredible pain went racing through his body. Starting at the base of the skull, zigzagging down his spine. He gasped, tried to turn around.

Another pain, even worse.

Someone had hit him, sapped him.

His feet left the deck, his trousers bunched around his crotch, his jacket popped open. Someone had grabbed him, lifted him off the deck.

Then he was in the fog. Part of it. Falling.

He tumbled down through the grayness and slammed into the black water hard.

The coldness of it grabbed at him, jabbing and knifing into all his soft spots.

He fought, flapped his arms, kicked.

Air. He was above the water, treading in the mist.

"Help, help! Man overboard! Man overboard!" someone was shouting.

He realized it was he.

18

SUCCESS.

He had the whole thing just about figured out. Barney knew who the killer was, and he'd realized the motive for the murder of Archie Judd and the attempt on his life.

Now if he could only stay alive long enough to do something about it.

"Hey! Man overboard! Help!"

Barney was losing touch with his fingers and toes. The chill water of the Sound was making him shiver and chatter. The fog was swirling around him.

Maybe, instead of waiting for the boat to realize he was gone, he ought to try to swim to shore.

You don't know where the shore is.

True, and he doubted he had the strength and stamina to swim all the way across to the Long Island side. How wide was the Sound hereabouts, anyway? One more simple everyday fact he didn't know.

"Help! M-m-man overboard!"

Barney maintained a determined treading, keeping himself afloat. The fog had built a wall around him. He couldn't hear the chuffing of the ferryboat or the blare of the music.

That damn jazz band. Everybody'd be listening to "King Porter Stomp" and "Jelly Roll Blues" and miss his shouts for help completely.

"Help! Man d-d-drowning!"

Something brushed his leg.

A shark?

Do they have sharks in this part of the Sound? There was another simple fact about Connecticut he ought to know but didn't. Knowledge such as that could come in handy.

Even if sharks were unknown in these waters, this might be a rogue. A killer fish who'd risk anything for a taste of—

"Barney, keep hollering!"

The voice got through the curtain of heavy mist.

"Texaco? Over here!"

The trick now was to keep the shark off until the rescuers reached him. You were supposed to stay perfectly still, not wave your arms or legs.

Problem with that was, he started to sink as soon as he quit paddling.

"Where, amigo?"

"Here!" He spit out salt water. "Over here!"

"There he is!" The nose of a rowboat, *Green-*

wich Queen in flaking green letters painted on it, emerged out of the fog.

Two crewmen, in jeans and pea jackets, were at the oars. A third crewman was at the prow of the boat, Texaco was crouched near him.

"You drunks," said the third man as he reached out with a grappling hook. "Catch hold of this."

Barney swam over to the side of the bobbing rowboat. He gripped the hook, the crewman caught his soggy coat back and hauled him into the craft. "I wasn't exactly drunk."

"Have a few drinks, decide to do stunts."

"Actually I was p—" Barney decided not to explain what he knew had happened. Because if he did, they'd ask him who. He wasn't quite ready to go into that yet. "I must've had a dizzy spell, don't know what caused it."

"You're probably allergic to the olives in martinis," said the crewman. "Back to the *Queen*, lads."

Texaco produced a folded blanket. "I heard you hollering off in the fog," he said as he unfurled the blanket and arranged it over his friend's sodden shoulders and back.

"How'd you hear? That music must've—"

"Fortunately they were taking a break when you took your plunge," he said. "I know you don't drink, so what really made you take this dip?"

Barney said, "I'll tell you later."

"Drunks," muttered the crewman.

"YOU SHOULDN'T BE DRIVING."

"There's no law against operating a motor vehicle while wrapped in a blanket."

The Volkswagen was clattering along a twisting Westport road, climbing toward Barney's cottage. He was at the wheel, hunched, still dripping some.

"I meant after being practically frozen and all, you—"

"I'm okay, and we're nearly home," he told Beth.

"Are you going to fill me in now," she asked, "on exactly what's been happening?"

"Somebody tried to kill me."

"That much I deduced on my own," she said. "Although for a brief spell I thought you'd maybe tried to kill yourself after encountering Tawny again. She was on board, did you know?"

Barney laughed. "I'm cured," he announced. "Details later."

"Cured of what?"

"Tawny," he said proudly. "That's one of the reasons I was hunting for you, to make you aware of my big breakthrough. She didn't affect me at all. Another reason I wanted to find you was to protect you."

"We thought I might be in danger and instead—"

"Were you really with Jape Easter?"

"As briefly as possible. He bought me a drink," she said. "Seemed simpler to suffer through one drink with him than have a long squabble over not. Mrs. Langendorf rescued me from him, but insisted on dragging me into the ladies' lounge where we had a long chat. She kept trying to convince me, laying on what must be the latest Independent Features party line, how lovely it would be if Archie retired on a pension. A generous pension."

"Langendorf brought up the same notion with me, promising a thousand bucks a week when I become the official 'Poor Little Pearl' artist."

"Did you...oh, we can talk business later. Tell me why someone tried to make you drown."

"The killer was along on the cruise." Barney guided his ancient car onto a dead-end lane. "He overheard me talking to Willis Folger and must've realized I was starting to put everything together. It was an improvised attempt, but he felt he had to give it a try."

"Do you know who killed my grandfather?"

"Yeah, I do."

"So who was it?"

"Jocko Pease," he answered as he pulled into his driveway.

"Jocko? What possible reason would he have for—"

"Look, the ferryboat made a special stop to land us." Barney, untangling himself from the blanket, opened his door. "The rest of them, including Jocko, won't be back on dry land for another two hours. That gives me enough time to get into dry clothes, make a couple of phone calls and then we'll drive over to Southport."

She eased out of her side of the VW. "What's in Southport?"

"I'm hoping there's some evidence," he said.

19

THE FOG WAS SPILLING across the beach, hiding most of the mansions that lined this Southport road.

"Who was that man you talked to in Ohio?" Beth asked.

Barney flipped his indicator for a left. "Grandson of Mrs. J.H. Coulthard. She was the widow of the long-defunct Colonel Coulthard," he answered. "See, at one time the colonel had one of the largest collections of original cartoon-art in America. Back when he died, though, in the late 1950s, not many people could foresee the day when original art would be one of the sought-after collectibles. Certainly old Mrs. Coulthard didn't dream there'd be cartoon museums and comic conventions."

"Or auctions at fancy Manhattan art galleries."

"Exactly, so she dumped her late husband's collection, which she'd always thought of as so much junk, in a loft over their barn. Although she couldn't bring herself to incinerate the collection, she was probably hoping time would get rid of all of it.''

"That's the collection Jocko Pease tracked down and bought about three or four months ago," said Beth. "I remember Willis Folger complaining about missing out on all those great pieces.''

Barney said, "Jocko wanted everyone, especially his insurance company, to think that. What he actually bought when he went out there to Ohio was some fifty rat-eaten, dirt-caked originals. The bulk of the collection had been destroyed by the Coulthard kids through the years. They used the originals to make airplanes, paper dolls, whatever. Some they gave away to other kids, a batch they sold on street corners in town for ten cents a sheet. Only reason there were even those fifty left is that the kids grew up and moved on.''

"That's sort of awful, all that valuable—"

"It didn't matter to Jocko," said Barney. "See, he only bought the dregs of the Colonel Coulthard collection to give himself a cover for what he was planning. If he hadn't tracked down the Coulthard heirs, he'd have come up with some other obscure collection from afar. What he had to do was mix several hundred fake originals in with that material. I found out tonight from William Coulthard that he signed several papers for Jocko, although he wasn't too sure what they all were. All he knows for certain is that Jocko gave him a thousand bucks for what he thought was a pile of junk. Jocko obviously must've gotten this rural lad to sign a faked inventory, one that would cover all the phony drawings, as well.''

"You're sure most of the collection was fake?''

"Had to be, otherwise everything that's been happening doesn't make any sense,'' he told her. ''The basic motive behind this was money, which Jocko needs badly. If the drawings were real he could've sold them off to collectors. They're not, though, and he couldn't risk that.''

"Where'd he get the fakes then?''

Barney pulled the VW to a stop on a tree-lined lane. ''He drew them.''

"Drew them? That would take—''

"You forget what a gifted ghost Jocko is.'' Turning off the ignition, Barney leaned back in his seat. ''He's filled in for a dozen artists the past few years. They all swear he's terrific. As the curator of a cartoon museum, as a legit collector himself, Jocko has a damn good idea of what valuable originals are still floating around. You've got to remember that until recently syndicates and magazines didn't think much of originals either. Tons of material were routinely burned, scrapped or hauled to the dumps. Until about fifteen years ago Maximus had a policy of shredding all the art after it was used.''

"So Jocko only forged drawings he was fairly certain didn't exist?''

"Right. He'd dig up a tear sheet of, say, a Little Nemo page from the early 1900s. After making an exact copy of it, he'd age the thing and maybe even nibble at the edges."

"Heck of a lot of work."

"The other call I made tonight was to Jocko's wife, former wife actually," he said. "She admitted he's been losing a lot of dough on this museum, not earning all that much as a free lance, either. Her friends quit backing him after the split. With the insurance money from the fire Jocko would have half a million dollars. More than enough to save his museum, pay his alimony and get himself out of hock."

"Still he had to copy hundreds of drawings."

"A Winsor McKay 'Little Nemo' goes for between seventy-five hundred and ten thousand dollars. He could probably knock one out in a week or less, so the potential payoff wasn't bad." Barney opened his door. "There's the museum down the hill there, with not a single light on." He slid out of the car.

The girl followed suit. "He'd need a year or more to turn out enough fakes, though."

"Could be Jocko's been doing it since he opened his cartoon museum. Initially he maybe toyed with the idea of slipping in a few fakes and selling them to collectors," he said. "That would be risky, because sooner or later someone might get suspicious. You burn the whole kaboodle at once and you're safer. Besides, you get all the money at once."

Beth took his hand. "Willis Folger appraised everything in the warehouse. He isn't in on this, is he?"

"Nope. Jocko is a damn good ghost. He can fake any style," said Barney. "Folger had only a few hours to go through hundreds of drawings, Jocko saw to that. Folger isn't an expert on every artist in the collection and, besides, he had no reason to suspect Jocko was parading a big pile of ringers by him. If Jocko had ever had to hang that stuff in the museum, someone might have tumbled."

"I remember Folger saying Jocko let him borrow a couple of the originals to study," said Beth. "Those, we can be sure, were some of the real ones."

"Yeah, exactly."

"Grandfather knew or suspected," she said, nodding her head slowly. "That was the reason for killing him."

"Jocko had picked a 'Pearl' page to fake that meant something special to Archie," said Barney. "It was the Sunday where he advertised his affair with Irene Loftin. When I listened to Archie's tapes, I heard him tell how the actress tore up that particular drawing and tossed it in his face."

"That's why grandfather had pulled the tape out of the box, to listen to it again."

"He wanted to refresh his memory, make absolutely sure. After all, he only knew Jocko as a jovial, backslapping fellow cartoonist,"

said Barney. "At that point, too, he didn't
know who had faked the page. Jocko might
have bought it in good faith, not realizing it was
a phony. So Archie, I'd guess, didn't say anything when he was at the museum."

"But then the warehouse burned down."

"Archie must've suspected then that all the
drawings might be fakes, which meant Jocko
was working a flimflam," said Barney. "Let's
work our way down there. I want to poke
around in the ruins."

"Grandfather must have telephoned Jocko
after he heard about the fire, hinted at what he
suspected."

They climbed down the grassy hillside, surrounded by drifting fog.

"I imagine old jovial Jocko pretended to be
surprised and shocked," said Barney. "He suggested a private meeting with Archie, so he
could explain the situation before Archie told
anybody else. Not at your house, but out in the
woods while Archie was taking his morning. . .
hey, the bandage!"

"Beg pardon?"

"That's another thing I've been trying to remember," he said. "When I met Jocko at the
N.A.G. banquet, he inquired about how Archie
was. Making small talk, he asked your dad if
Archie's hand was better."

"Grandfather did hurt his hand before he was
killed."

"Yeah, but not before he went to the museum. In those damn pictures Folger took both his hands are clean," Barney told her. "The only way Jocko could've known about the injury is by seeing Archie at a later time. That was the morning he killed him."

The fog was brushed away by a sudden gust of night wind. The wreckage of the museum warehouse loomed up directly ahead of them.

"Jocko is our other prowler, too," said the girl. "He's been hanging around, trying to find out about grandfather."

"He must have been certain Archie was dead, but then there's no mention of it and you people are acting like the old man is only down with the flu," said Barney. "By now he must suspect you're lying, but he's not sure what shape Archie is in. Since nobody's blown the whistle on him, he has to assume Archie is in no condition to talk. He doesn't know how long that state will last, so he has got to get another crack at the old man. Meanwhile he overhears me talking to Folger tonight. Sounds like I must know something, too. He decided to try a little accident on me."

"I'm glad it didn't work," she said quietly. "What are we supposed to find here?"

They halted at the edge of the burned-out building. The odor of damp, charred wood was strong.

"As much as Jocko would like to get rid of all

this, I don't think he'd dare take away the fragments of the burned drawings until the insurance people are absolutely through," Barney said. "That might just make them suspicious."

"We're hunting for fragments of faked drawings?"

"Yeah, with a few scraps we should be able to prove the forgery angle," he answered, taking from his pocket the pencil flashlight he'd picked up at his cottage. "Drawing paper and ink they used fifty, sixty years ago isn't like the stuff we use today, for one thing. There's nobody in the museum proper and Jocko is still at sea, so we can have our scavenger hunt undisturbed."

The girl watched him probing with the beam of the light. "It'll all come out now, won't it?" she said. "What father and I did, everything."

He stepped over into the blackened wreckage of the building. "It has to, Beth," he said.

20

"REMIND ME not to have myself cremated."
Squatting, Barney arranged the sooty, black-edged fragments of original drawings on the newspapers Beth was spreading on the floor of her grandfather's studio.

"It's not a winning scent, moldering ashes."

"Looks like we got enough samples to have tested," he said. "Here's two nearly complete panels of 'Little Nemo,' a quarter of a page of 'Dick Tracy' from the thirties and, which is the greatest find, almost a third of a Sunday 'Poor Little Pearl.'"

"Some of these might be real."

Barney shook his head. "Nope, Jocko wouldn't burn a real 'Little Nemo,'" he said. "In fact, once Folger and the insurance folks saw the collection, he more than likely stashed most of the authentic drawings away in the museum somewhere."

Sitting on the edge of a wicker chair and brushing a smear of soot from her cheek with the heel of her hand, Beth said, "How do we go about this, what's the first step? I suppose we have to tell the police about—"

"First we contact Jocko's insurance company," Barney told her. "When we prove what Jocko's been up to, they'll be on our side. Before we call the cops I want to have as many influential allies on our side as possible."

"Still going to be one heck of a mess."

"A mess, sure," he acknowledged. "Though not as vast as it could've been. With the insurance company doing some investigating of their own, it'll be easier to get the police to think about Jocko as the murderer of Archie Judd."

"No matter how many people are on our side, we can't get around the fact father and I tried to cover up a death."

"When's Russ due back from Philly?"

"Next week sometime. The 'Pearl' musical people were vague as to how long they'd need him."

Rubbing ashes and mud off the crystal, Barney checked his watch. "After midnight. We were rummaging around longer than I thought," he said. "Even so, you better call your dad and tell him to get back home. We're going to need him to work up some clout. We'll need your attorney working for us, and Russ should be able, as one of Westport's wealthier citizens, to butter up a few selectmen and town fathers."

"Archie was the wealthy one, but father does have some influential friends. I don't know how they'll feel about the idea of our keeping grandfather stuffed in the freezer," she said quietly. "It really was a crackpot idea from the—"

"With any luck we'll get you both a medal for preserving the evidence of a vicious crime," he said. "What we have to emphasize when we start telling our story tomorrow is that we're handing a big-time swindler and murderer over to the authorities."

"Everybody's still going to think dad and I behaved like—"

"Most of them will identify with you," he assured her. "Now call your father, tell him to get back here fast. Maybe we can phone your family lawyer tonight, too. Tomorrow I'll find out who insured Jocko's collection of—"

"What's all that dang noise down there? Where the devil is my nightcap?"

Beth, eyes wide, stood up. "My god, Barney!"

There was a thumping from upstairs. The voice continued with, "Going to count ten and then I'm going to yell a blue streak!"

Barney, dodging the spread-out tatters of drawings, ran out of the studio and into the main hallway.

"Evening, chump."

Turning, he saw Jocko Pease planted just to the left of the studio doorway. The big shaggy

man held a .38 revolver and was chuckling softly.

"Tell her to come on out here," he suggested
in a low voice.

"So you can shoot her, too?"

"I can drop you right here and go in and drag
her out," Jocko said. "Less messy this way. Call
her."

"Beth, you better come here."

"What is it? What's wrong?"

"Just come here."

She walked slowly out into the hallway,
looked from Barney's face to the gun in Jocko's
hairy fist. "We thought you were still on the
boat."

"Naw, that docked an hour ago," said Jocko.
"I came right over, anxious to see what you two
were up to. When it turned out nobody was
home, I let myself in and have been doing some
interesting exploring around."

"You found the tapes," said Barney.

"Better than that, I found poor old Archie,"
said Jocko. "Really a relief to find out the old
bastard's actually dead."

"You did kill him," said Beth, "met him on
the road and smashed—"

"We're talking about half a million dollars
here," cut in Jocko. "You think I was going to
let one old fart keep me from that? He wouldn't
have lived that much longer anyhow, I just gave
him a head start."

"You planning to help us next?" said Barney, eyes on the gun.

"Was hoping to get you earlier tonight, Barney," Jocko told him. "But this'll work even better. You and Bethany came here after your dip in the Sound, then she, seeing you were still in shaky shape, decided to drive you home. Trouble is, she's not at all familiar with a Volks, being used to sporting around in a much fancier machine. Taking a shortcut over the back roads behind this place, she lost control. Terrible shame, such a pretty young girl and such a talented young guy. Life can be rough sometimes. They find you both cooked to a turn, the car smacked into a tree and burned."

"You're fond," said Barney, "of burning cars."

"It's a snap to set one on fire and very tough to prove any funny business," said Jocko, grinning. "That's why I used my Datsun as a fuse for the sad fire at the museum warehouse. Old wooden building like that, once you get a good blaze going, there's little chance to save anything. Real pity."

Beth edged nearer to Barney. "Did you really forge all those drawings?"

Jocko said, "Damn right I did. Shame, in a way, I couldn't have displayed them. Some of my best ghost work. I did an especially nice Billy De Beck 'Barney Google' Sunday page, complete with Spark Plug the race horse. Beautiful job."

"So much effort up in smoke," said Beth.

"I'm getting half a million for it," said Jocko. "Take me twenty lousy years working in my chosen profession to earn that."

Barney said, "You'll never collect it."

"From what I overheard, you and Bethany haven't told Russ yet. Meaning, once you two have your tragic little accident, I'm home free."

"Folger is suspicious now," said Barney.

"Folger is a jerk. Once you're dead he'll forget."

"Texaco knows, too."

"Who? That greaseball?"

"I told him tonight, when he helped pull me out of the Sound," said Barney. "You can't kill Folger, Texaco—"

"Nice try, but no cigar." Jocko laughed. "I happened to have had a chat with your chicano buddy after you and Bethany left the boat. He's not that good an actor, he doesn't suspect me of a damn thing."

"What's to stop the police from searching this house once we're dead?" persisted Barney. "They'll find Archie's body, tie the—"

"Naw, they won't. Because after I take care of you folks, I'm going to bury Archie off in the boonies someplace," explained Jocko. "Let Russ worry about explaining that." He gestured at the front door with his gun hand. "Any more bluffs you'd like to run?"

"Why not quit while you—"

"I don't quit until I get the half million. Now march on out that—"

All at once a loud knocking commenced on the front door.

For a few seconds Jocko turned his eyes toward the door.

And during those few seconds Barney leaped. He chopped at Jocko's wrist with a flat-handed blow.

Jocko howled, his grip on the gun loosening.

Barney chopped again, the .38 fell free, thwacked onto the floor.

The next chop caught the shaggy man in the throat. He swung a wild blow, gasping in air.

Barney hit him twice more.

The big man's knees snapped together, his toes pointing toward each other. He was able to take two wobbling steps in Barney's direction before toppling.

As he fell, Barney kicked him once in the side of the head.

Jocko landed out cold.

Rubbing his palm along the side of his hand, Barney stood away from the fallen man. He hunched slightly, breathing in a rough uneven way. "You better," he said in a dry voice, "answer the door."

"Oh. . . ." Beth, skirting the sprawled Jocko, crossed and opened the heavy front door of the mansion a few inches.

"Excuse the banging, Beth, but I couldn't

find the bell in this fog," said Texaco. "I decided to drop by to see how Barney's doing. He wasn't at his place, so I—"

"Come in, come in," she invited.

The curly-haired little cartoonist entered and noticed Jocko. "Very unusual throw rug you have," he said.

"There's an interesting story behind how we got it," said Barney.

21

CROUCHED AT HIS DRAWING BOARD, Texaco was filling in blacks on a page with broad sweeps of a felt marker. Sensing Barney's arrival, he straightened up, his bones making several small cricking sounds. "I was anticipating your exit would be horizontal, amigo," he said, "accompanied by considerable ferocious bellowing."

"Carlotsky took the news in a manly fashion." Barney sat in the chair Warloff had once occupied. "Actually, quitting things has turned out to be a lot easier than I anticipated."

Texaco stroked the stubble on his chin with the blank end of his marker. "You really are going ahead with your foolhardy plan?"

"Yep. I just turned in my last Human Beast job. Yesterday I finished up my 'Poor Little Pearl' daily."

The curly-haired cartoonist said, "I admire your courage, since total and absolute freelancing is an awesome way of life."

"There's a possibility Benevolent Mutual, the

folks who were going to have to pay Jocko half
a million bucks, will pay me some kind of honor-
arium for exposing his scam. And I was able to
save some money out of the 'Pearl' salary. I
really think I can get along until I'm ready to
start hustling commercial accounts again."

"All the mess I walked into the other eve's
been cleaned up?" asked Texaco. "The Manhattan sheets, even the revered *Post*, have been
less than generous with the lurid details."

"Russell Judd was able to pull some strings.
The police have Jocko Pease to hang the actual
murder on, the insurance company is going to
save all their money," said Barney. "The ac-
tions of Beth and her father after they found
the body are being overlooked and probably
won't leak out. Although, since Jocko's being
held for murdering Archie Judd, his lawyers
may try to bring that stuff out eventually. Right
now Jocko has to worry about a murder charge,
the arson and fraud charges and, possibly,
they'll also try to charge him with attempted
murder."

"For giving you the heave-ho into the
Sound."

"Yeah, but that charge is way down the list."

"One thing I admire about the chap," said
Texaco. "He did come up with a nifty way to
make money as a cartoonist. Half a million for a
year's work is nice."

Barney said, "The whole damn scheme might

have worked if Archie hadn't remembered what had happened to that drawing, and if Folger hadn't been so gung ho about dragging him out to see the stuff in the museum warehouse."

"Too bad Jocko couldn't have avoided that little private showing."

"I'm sure he wanted to, but he couldn't risk making Folger suspicious. He decided to risk it, probably feeling an old man like Archie wouldn't know if the drawings were fake or not after all these years. And Jocko's fakes were damn good; he even printed up his own little syndicate copyright stickers to put on most of them."

"Ah, but he didn't reckon that true love never dies," said Texaco with a less than sincere sigh. "I've never had any of my drawings tossed in my face, even by Carlotsky. Yet I've immortalized numerous of my ladies in the pages of 'Flaming Death.' Princess Lomalinda of Venus, in the current yarn, for instance, is a true pen portrait of that girl I was telling you about who is the spitting image of Wanda Hendrix of yore. Although it occurs to me she may not realize it since I had, bound to conform to Maximus policy, to endow the princess with an enormous set of hinkers."

"Even though I'm not going to be working for Maximus anymore," Barney said, "we ought to keep in touch."

"That's what they all say," said Texaco. "Once you graduate, though, you won't come back."

"Sure, I will. Besides which, you saved our lives the other night. That links us up forever."

"I save you folks in typical Texaco fashion, by stumbling into something," he said. "What's going to happen to 'Poor Little Pearl'? I hear the syndicate is looking for a new artist, but who's going to write it?"

Barney grinned. "Russ Judd is going to keep on."

"He is?" Texaco put down his marker. "After he tried to pull the wool over Independent Features' eyes? Tried to keep getting his share of the 'Pearl' loot? I assumed he'd be drummed out of the corps."

"That's what Langendorf wanted to do," Barney said. "It turns out, however, that everybody thinks Russ's doctoring of the *Poor Little Pearl* musical is what turned it into a smash. Thing opened night before last in Philadelphia to rave reviews."

"And so?"

"Certain of the money people behind the musical are very fond of Russ. They've made it clear he's to keep writing the strip and stay handy for rewriting when they hit New York with the show next month."

"Something like that swayed the coldhearted bunch up at Independent Features?"

"Couple of the backers are of considerable influence here in the East. One, matter of fact, hinted Langendorf might end up in the East River if he was nasty to Russ."

"Aha, that kind of money. You can't argue with that," said the little cartoonist. "If Judd's going to keep on writing the strip, you could keep drawing it. Right?"

"Probably," admitted Barney. "Except this seemed like a good time to quit. I've cured myself of Tawny, I solved a murder, I missed getting killed myself. Time to try scrambling up to the next plateau."

"What about Beth?"

Barney steepled the fingers of his right hand on Warloff's abandoned drawing board. "She hasn't made up her mind what she's going to do," he said.

"What are her options?"

"She can stay on with her father, managing the affairs of the strip," Barney answered. "Even though they've lost their fifty percent of the proceeds, Independent is still going to pay Russ something like fifty thousand a year."

"I suppose two people can scrape by on that in these troubled times, if they skip a lunch here and there," remarked Texaco. "What was the other choice?"

"I like Beth."

"Careful now, amigo, that's pretty strong language."

"Okay, I love her and I asked her to . . . well, share my life."

"In your humble cottage?"

"For now, yeah."

"This was a marriage proposal?"

"I'm still not legally unhooked from Tawny. Until I am Beth and I would just live together."

"Wow," said Texaco. "The sexual revolution comes to cartoonland."

Barney grinned, saying nothing.

Texaco picked up his black marker. "Did she accept?"

"She's thinking about it."

Texaco said, "You knew about Archie being dead for quite a while, didn't you?"

"A few weeks, or at least I suspected."

"You didn't tell anyone?"

"I had to find out what had really happened."

"A tough sort of secret to keep to yourself."

Barney stood up. "As I grow older, I seem to be getting better at keeping my mouth shut." He eased to the doorway.

"Good luck on all fronts. Okay?"

"Okay." Barney left.

22

HIS PHONE RANG again.

Barney stayed beside his open portfolio, forcing himself to wait three rings before dashing across his studio to answer. "Hello."

"What's this I've been hearing about you, old buddy?"

"I give up, Ty, what?"

"That you have made several major changes in your life. But I sense a note of disappointment in your voice. Have I called at the wrong time?"

"I've been expecting a call, an important one. But since I got home from New York this afternoon Bud Heinz phoned, Sears called to let me know about their washrag sale, Willis Folger called to remind me he wants to sell my old originals, the *Fairpress* asked for an interview, Jerry Marcus called and now you."

"For a confirmed loner, you're right in the middle of a social whirl," said Banner in his slightly blurred voice. "My latest wife, the lovely Trish, wants me to beg you to drop over for an informal dinner this evening."

"Thanks, but I have to stick here tonight." Outside his cottage the day was waning, a soft darkness slowly replacing it. "I'm trying to put together a new portfolio."

"Then the rumors are true, you are planning to abandon cartooning?"

"I've abandoned already."

"A wise decision, old buddy."

"Some kind of decision, anyway. It's what I want to do."

Banner said, "You may recall that when I first mentioned the ghosting job to you, I guaranteed you it would change your life."

"Yep, a very accurate prediction."

After clearing his throat, Banner said, "You could have stayed on with 'Poor Little Pearl,' couldn't you?"

"Could have, except this seemed like a good place to get off."

"I hear Jape Easter's the most likely candidate to take over the waif."

Laughing, Barney said, "I had a feeling he'd go after the job."

"I think you owe me a full account of this whole business," Banner told him. "There are few murders in my circle anymore, and I like to savor the details of each one."

"Maybe later," said Barney. "Give my best to your loved ones."

"Righto, I won't keep your phone tied up any longer," said Banner. "Listen, though, Barney, if you need anything to help relaunch you into the illustration thing, let me know. I can even provide a modest loan if need be.''

"Appreciate that, Ty. So long.''

Hanging up, Barney returned to the portfolio lying open on the throw rug. He was going to need half a dozen new samples at least to liven this up.

Jape Easter, huh? Had Beth helped select him, put in a good word? Maybe their old romance would get going again.

Let's strive to rid ourselves of such goofy thoughts.

He settled cross-legged onto his studio floor, turning the acetate pages of the portfolio and studying each sample illustration.

The day went completely away, darkness closed in on him.

Barney was stretching for the cord of the nearest lamp when he heard a faint sound that might be a knocking.

Dashing into the living room of his cottage, he opened the front door wide.

Beth was standing on the threshold, a small suitcase held tight in both hands. "I've made up my mind," she said.

Be a detective.
See if you can solve . . .

Raven House
MINUTE
MYSTERY #4

On the following page is Raven House
MINUTE MYSTERY #4, "A Sound Sleeper."

Every month each Raven House book will feature a
MINUTE MYSTERY, a unique little puzzler designed
to let *you* do the sleuthing!

U.S. (except Arizona) residents may check the answer
by calling **1-800-528-1404** anytime from March 1 to
May 15, 1982. U.S. residents may also obtain the solution
by writing anytime during or after this period to:

Raven House MINUTE MYSTERY
1440 South Priest Drive
Tempe, AZ 85281

Canadian residents, please write to the following
address:

Raven House MINUTE MYSTERY
649 Ontario Street
Stratford, Ontario N5A 6W2

A SOUND SLEEPER

Professor Fordney's attention was attracted by a suspicious-looking bulge in the right pocket of an obviously expensive camel's-hair overcoat, which was thrown carelessly over Skamp's green coat.

"That yours?" he asked John London.

"Yes, sir. You see...."

"Just a moment," interrupted the professor. A rather sheepish grin spread over his face when he found the bulge in the coat was made by a large peppermint candy cane. Examining the green coat, a sudden thought struck him. Perhaps that cane did have some significance!

He had already seen the body of Henry Skamp lying on the floor of the one-room apartment. Skamp had been stabbed.

"All right," Fordney nodded to London, "continue."

"Last night Henry came home a bit drunk, woke me up, and when I refused to listen to him tell about his love affair, he flung his coat on that chair and lay down beside me fully dressed. I was tired and went right back to sleep. When I awoke this morning—around nine o'clock—I found him lying there dead and called the police."

"You heard no sound after you went to sleep the second time, and you disturbed nothing?" the professor inquired.

"No—I was dead tired."

"How long have you two been roommates?"

"Oh, quite a while. About two years. I forgot to tell you that three months ago Henry lost his job and he's been brooding ever since."

"H'mm...." Fordney pondered a moment. "You're lying, London. I'm holding you on suspicion!"

How did the professor know London was lying?

Raven House Mysteries

An exciting opportunity to read some of the finest in mystery fiction!

As a Raven House subscriber you will receive every month 4 action-filled, spine-chilling mystery novels, superbly written by talented authors who are all members of the prestigious MYSTERY WRITERS OF AMERICA.
You may cancel your subscription whenever you wish.
Should you decide to stop your order, just let us know and we'll cancel all further shipments.

COMPLETE AND MAIL THIS COUPON TODAY!